Carissa looked around for a weapon.

The gleam of metal on the windowsill caught her eye. She picked up the old cigar tube she'd found when she arrived at the lodge, an idea growing.

Careful to avoid creaking floorboards, she reached her bedroom and felt her heartbeat quicken. The intruder was in there.

Through a small gap in the doorway she saw a man a head taller than she. She swallowed. Lord, he was big—wide at the shoulders and narrow everywhere else. His aristocratic profile tugged at her memory, but before she could pinpoint the reason, she decided it was now or never.

She pushed open the door, moved up behind the man and pressed the cigar tube into his back with all the force she could muster. "Don't move. I have a gun, and I know how to use it."

Dear Reader,

Ring in the holidays with Silhouette Romance! Did you know our books make terrific stocking stuffers? What a wonderful way to remind your friends and family of the power of love!

This month, everyone is in store for some extraspecial goodies. Diana Palmer treats us to her LONG, TALL TEXANS title, *Lionhearted* (#1631), in which the last Hart bachelor ties the knot in time for the holidays. And Sandra Steffen wraps up THE COLTONS series about the secret Comanche branch, with *The Wolf's Surrender* (#1630). Don't miss the grand family reunion to find out how your favorite Coltons are doing!

Then, discover if an orphan's wish for a family—and snow on Christmas—comes true in Cara Colter's heartfelt *Guess Who's Coming for Christmas?* (#1632). Meanwhile, wedding bells are the last thing on school nurse Kate Ryerson's mind—or so she thinks—in Myrna Mackenzie's lively romp, *The Billionaire Borrows a Bride* (#1634).

And don't miss the latest from popular Romance authors Valerie Parv and Donna Clayton. Valerie Parv brings us her mesmerizing tale, *The Marquis and the Mother-To-Be* (#1633), part of THE CARRAMER LEGACY in which Prince Henry's heirs discover the perils of love! And Donna Clayton is full of shocking surprises with *The Doctor's Pregnant Proposal* (#1635), the second in THE THUNDER CLAN series about a family of proud, passionate people.

We promise more exciting new titles in the coming year. Make it your New Year's resolution to read them all!

Happy reading!

Mary-Theresa Hussey

Mary-Theresa Hussey
Senior Editor

Please address questions and book requests to:
Silhouette Reader Service
U.S.: 3010 Walden Ave., P.O. Box 1325, Buffalo, NY 14269
Canadian: P.O. Box 609, Fort Erie, Ont. L2A 5X3

The Marquis and the Mother-To-Be

Valerie Parv

SILHOUETTE *Romance*

Published by Silhouette Books

America's Publisher of Contemporary Romance

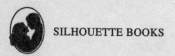

SILHOUETTE BOOKS

ISBN 0-373-19633-4

THE MARQUIS AND THE MOTHER-TO-BE

Copyright © 2002 by Valerie Parv

This edition published by arrangement with Harlequin Books S.A.

® and TM are trademarks of Harlequin Books S.A., used under license. Trademarks indicated with ® are registered in the United States Patent and Trademark Office, the Canadian Trade Marks Office and in other countries.

Visit Silhouette at www.eHarlequin.com

Printed in U.S.A.

VALERIE PARV

lives and breathes romance and has even written a guide to being romantic, crediting her cartoonist husband of nearly thirty years as her inspiration. As a former buffalo and crocodile hunter in Australia's Northern Territory, he's ready-made hero material, she says.

When not writing her novels and nonfiction books, or speaking about romance on Australian radio and television, Valerie enjoys dollhouses, being a *Star Trek* fan and playing with food (in cooking, that is). Valerie agrees with actor Nichelle Nichols, who said, "The difference between fantasy and fact is that fantasy simply hasn't happened yet."

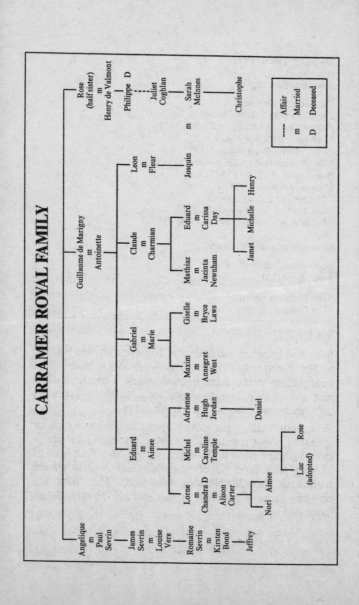

CARRAMER ROYAL FAMILY

Guillaume de Marigny
m
Antoinette

Rose (half sister)
m
Henry de Valmont

Philippe D ----- Juliet Coghlan

Sarah McInnes

Christophe

Angelique
m
Paul Sevrin

Eduard
m
Aimee

Gabriel
m
Marie

Claude
m
Charmian

Leon
m
Fleur

James Sevrin
m
Louise Vere

Romaine Sevrin
m
Kirsten Bond

Jeffrey

Lorne
m
Chandra D

Michel
m
Caroline Temple

Adrienne
m
Hugh Jordan

Maxim
m
Annegret West

Giselle
m
Bryce Laws

Mathiaz
m
Jacinta Newnham

Eduard
m
Carissa Day

Josquin

Alison Carter

Luc (adopted)

Rose

Daniel

Jamet   Michelle   Henry

Nori   Aimee

-----	Affair
m	Married
D	Deceased

Prologue

Excitement gripped Carissa Day as she followed the real estate agent through an overgrown garden toward a rambling house. The pleasantly weathered timber walls, bay windows and shingle roof made the building look at ease in the rain-forest setting. The prospect of living twenty minutes' drive from the nearest town only added to its charm, she decided.

"Are you sure about the price, Mr. Hass?" she asked, concerned at how close she was to losing her heart. The lodge so exactly fitted her dream of the bed-and-breakfast place she wanted to establish that she had to remind herself it wouldn't be a picnic. Taming the garden alone would keep her busy for some time.

"I'm quite sure," the agent said in his elusive accent. "This used to be a country retreat for a wealthy family, but it hasn't been used for two years. The owner died nine months ago after a long illness, and the new owner instructed me to sell it off. He's in the

Carramer Royal Navy and away a lot, so doesn't want to be encumbered by a country house.''

"Who was the owner?''

Hass hesitated before saying, "It was someone called de Valmont. He willed the property to his nephew, my client.''

She had met the agent by chance at the Monarch Hotel in Tricot, where she had based herself so she could look at a property in the area. She had told the agent that she was Australian and had lived in Carramer when she was fifteen with her brother and diplomat father. She had never visited this area, but the name of the former owner was familiar. "Aren't the de Valmonts part of the royal family?''

The agent looked away. "A lot of Carramer families claim royal connections.''

She thought of the de Marigny brothers she had known when she was a teenager. They hadn't claimed to be royal. They were the real thing. Mathiaz was a baron and Eduard was a marquis. For a time, she had believed she was in love with Eduard. Even now, a flutter in her stomach accompanied the thought of the handsome young royal.

He wasn't the reason she had chosen to return to Carramer after her father died, she assured herself. Long over that teenage crush, she was only interested in the house's royal connections as a potential attraction for visitors.

Hass led her along a gravel path to a back door. "The house comes with many of the original furnishings and fittings.''

"That will help. Most of my possessions are in storage.''

His eyes gleamed, and she regretted letting him see

how interested she was in the house before she had set foot in it. "Of course it needs a lot of work," she added, trying to sound like less of a pushover.

"The condition of the house is reflected in the price, which is negotiable."

She was pleased to hear it. Even at a bargain price, she would be straining her budget to buy the lodge. Hass had confided that the new owner was willing to provide a mortgage with generous terms. But after paying the substantial down payment Hass had named, she wouldn't have much of her inheritance left for redecorating.

She noticed that the agent was having trouble with the lock, which was broken. He gave her an apologetic smile. "The keys have been lost. That's why I'm taking you in through the kitchen." Seeing her frown, he added, "There are sturdy bolts on the inside for nighttime security. If you decide to buy, there's a locksmith in Tricot who can fit new locks for you."

"I'll look into it."

So much for objectivity, she thought. She was already sold and they both knew it. She must have had a premonition about the lodge, because she carried a bank check for the deposit in her purse, having taken Hass's advice and withdrawn the money before making the inspection. Now she had seen the place, she hated the idea of anyone else snapping it up.

She didn't try to pretend that she wasn't delighted with the inside of the house. The old-fashioned kitchen was large with a scrubbed timber table in the center, perfect for preparing the home-cooked meals she intended to offer guests. Beyond was a dining room with a vaulted, timber-lined ceiling, a comfortable living room with old but elegant furniture arranged around a massive stone fireplace and five bedrooms in two wings off a wide gallery hallway. Three of them had en suite bathrooms with traditional claw-footed baths and brass fittings.

As Hass led her back along the hallway, Carissa inspected the portraits lining the walls. ''These look like originals.''

''They are excellent reproductions, aren't they? They come with the house.''

As they returned to the kitchen, she took a deep breath. ''How negotiable do you think the new owner is willing to be?''

Chapter One

Eduard de Marigny, Marquis of Merrisand, wondered if he could recognize the terrain well enough to set the helicopter down on the landing pad behind Tiga Falls Lodge. Over two years had passed since his last visit, and he hadn't piloted his own chopper then. The estate had belonged to his uncle, Prince Henry, and they had driven in a royal cavalcade from Perla, capital city of Valmont Province, a hundred and sixty miles away by road.

Strange to think of the house belonging to him now, Eduard thought, looking down at the rambling timber building nestled in the greenery. Eduard couldn't honestly say he missed old Prince Henry, who had ruled the province with an iron hand. Eduard's cousin, Josquin, had succeeded Henry as Crown Regent until the heir, Prince Christophe, came of age. Josquin managed to do an excellent job of running the province while being far easier to get along with than Henry had been.

Still, Henry had kept their branch of the royal family

on its toes, insisting that titles and protocol were strictly observed. He had approved of his nephew joining the Carramer Royal Navy, especially when Eduard had gained his commission, but the old prince had disapproved of the informality Eduard permitted among the men under his command.

Eduard wondered what Henry would have made of the Australians he'd met during the last few months while he was seconded to the Australian Navy, on exercises off the coast of Queensland. On duty, military protocol had been observed, but off duty, he had been Ed, or "your lordship" when the Australians wanted to poke fun at him, which had been often.

Now he was home for a few weeks at least, he intended to spend his accumulated leave at the lodge, assessing his future. His brother, Mathiaz, had offered him a government position, but Eduard didn't see himself as the administrative type. Tiga Falls had beckoned and with it, some serious decision-making to be done.

He spiraled in on the position of the landing pad, almost lost among the trees from this height, but gradually he made it out behind the lodge. A crosswind buffeted the small craft, so Eduard orbited until he was sure of a safe landing, then took her in.

The helicopter settled gently, and Eduard stayed in the pilot's seat until the rotors stopped spinning. He half expected Henry's staff to rush out to meet him, but they had either retired or taken up other positions with the family when the lodge was closed up after Henry became ill. Mathiaz had offered to send staff to open things up, but Eduard preferred to take care of himself for the time being, having acquired the habit in the navy.

"Does the word *security* mean anything to you?" his brother had asked pointedly.

"I didn't have minders in the navy. I don't need them at the lodge."

Mathiaz hadn't liked Eduard going off into the wilderness without at least one member of the Royal Protection Detail in attendance, but he hadn't insisted. Eduard looked forward to the solitude, having had little enough of it in his life, either as a member of the royal family or in the military.

He hefted his duffel bag over his shoulder and climbed out of the helicopter, looking around with satisfaction. Henry couldn't have left him anything that pleased him more. He decided to go inside and look around first. There was plenty of time to bring the rest of his stuff in later.

The key he tried to insert into the front-door lock didn't fit. He frowned, trying some of the other keys. None of them worked. With a snort of annoyance, he walked around to the kitchen door, coming up short at the sight of a car parked behind the house. Had Mathiaz sent someone anyway?

On closer inspection, Eduard found the vehicle unlocked. It was a few years old and looked barely roadworthy. The only clue to the driver's identity was a straw sun hat trimmed with silk flowers lying on the front seat. Curious.

The key he tried in the kitchen-door lock didn't work either. Experimentally, he turned the handle and to his surprise, the door swung open. What was going on here?

He had expected the place to smell musty after being unused for more than two years, but the air was surprisingly fresh. If he hadn't known better, he would swear he could smell baking. Just as well he didn't believe in ghosts, because the place was starting to seem haunted.

The ghost was young and female, he decided, as he ducked under a row of lacy undergarments hanging from an improvised line in the kitchen. Evidently she hadn't gotten around to haunting the lodge's laundry yet.

The kitchen was vast, as befitted the size of the lodge. He saw no sign of the ghost herself, but evidence of her presence was everywhere, not only in the line of laundry, but also in the washed plates and cup neatly stacked beside the sink.

He left his bag in the kitchen and made his way along the gallery hallway to the bedroom wings. This part of the lodge was also occupied, he found to his annoyance. The novelty was fast wearing off, as he saw that someone had made herself at home in the room he usually preferred. It looked out onto the distant hills, although the view was obscured by overgrown trees now. He planned to attack them while he was here.

Evidently his ghost liked the room for the same reason he did, because the drapes were drawn right back and the window was open, letting a ginger-scented breeze into the room. Whoever his ghost was, she was tidy, and had good taste in bedrooms, although she was fairly lax when it came to security.

He froze as a hard cylindrical object bored into the small of his back and a female voice said, "Don't move. I have a gun and I know how to use it."

Returning to the lodge after her walk, Carissa Day heard the helicopter before she saw it. She watched it swoop low then disappear behind the tree line, heading toward the township of Tricot on the other side of the river. She wondered what had brought it here.

She hoped there wasn't a medical emergency in the town. When she had made an appointment with the local doctor soon after she arrived, he had explained that urgent medical cases had to be flown to the hospital in Casmira, some fifty miles south. He had plainly disapproved of a foreigner taking up residence so far from help when she was pregnant.

She had told him that apart from being plagued by morning sickness, which he'd assured her would pass as her pregnancy progressed, she was fine.

"Is your husband joining you?" he had asked.

She had taken a firm hold of her temper before saying, "No."

To his credit the doctor hadn't pressed the issue and she hadn't explained further. This was *her* baby and no one else's. Now they had the lodge as a home and future source of income, they had everything they needed.

She stopped and stretched, pressing both hands into the small of her back. She had assigned herself a daily walk partly for exercise but mostly because she was in love with the lush rain-forest countryside surrounding her new home, and wanted to explore every inch of it while she still could.

Now the helicopter rotors had stopped beating, she could hear only birdsong and the whisper of leaves. Perfect peace. Her eyes misted in appreciation of the beauty around her.

A fragment of Yeats came into her mind: "Was there on earth a place so dear..." She might have been born in Australia but she loved Carramer with a fierceness that surprised her at times. Her baby was going to love it, too. She couldn't imagine a more healthy, nurturing environment in which to bring a child into the world than right here.

She was determined to do better as a sole parent than her father had done. Graeme Day had been too preoccupied with the demands of diplomatic life to accommodate his children's emotional needs. Their father had treated her and Jeffrey like miniature adults, expecting them to adapt to the different places they were dropped into, as easily as he did himself.

Sometimes they had and sometimes they hadn't. To Carissa, Carramer was the only posting where she had felt at home. She had been heartbroken when her father announced they were returning to Australia. Too young to remain in the country alone, she had vowed to return as soon as she got the chance.

Her brother had thought she was crazy. "Give me the bright lights, big city" was Jeff's motto. Carramer had its share of cities, too, but Carissa felt more at home in the lush, tropical regions barely touched by the hand of civilization.

She sighed. Home still needed a lot of work if she was to turn it into the bed-and-breakfast haven of her dreams. It wouldn't happen by itself. Time she got back and made herself useful.

When she emerged from the rain forest into the clearing, the first thing she noticed was the kitchen door standing ajar. She knew she had closed it when she went out, had even been tempted to lock it until she asked herself who on earth she expected to break in here.

It looked as if she was going to find out.

Skirting the car, which appeared untouched, she peered around the door before going in. The kitchen was empty. Her laundry had dried on the makeshift line, and the smell of her morning's baking lingered in the air. But it was overlaid with a pine-and-leather scent that hadn't been there when she left. Silently she stripped the line of clothes, dumping them on a chair. If she had to make a fast exit, she didn't want obstacles in her way.

She looked around for a weapon. A rolling pin would do the job but might be turned against her, she remembered from the self-defense lessons she'd taken as a teenager. The gleam of metal on the windowsill caught her eye. She picked up the old cigar tube she'd found when she arrived. She turned it over in her hands, an idea growing in her.

The pine scent led her down the hallway. Careful to avoid those floorboards she knew were prone to creak, she reached her bedroom and felt her heartbeat quicken. Someone was in the room. Common sense told her to call the police in Tricot. But what were the odds they could reach her before the intruder heard her talking and came to investigate?

For now she was on her own.

Through the three-finger gap in the doorway she saw the man look around. He was a head taller than she was, with chestnut hair cut in a military style. He half turned and she swallowed. Lord, he was big, wide at shoulder and hip and narrow everywhere else. His aristocratic profile tugged at her memory, but before she could pinpoint the reason, he turned away again.

She took stock of his clothing so she would be able to describe him to the police when she could safely contact them. White shirt, the sleeves rolled back over tanned forearms, open at the neck. The shirt was tucked into snug-fitting denims held up by a plaited leather belt slung cowboy-style around his hips. As he moved to the window, the gleam of his boots jarred her. What kind of prowler polished his boots to a mirror shine?

Now or never, she told herself, pushing the door all the way open. Without giving herself time to think, she moved up behind him and pressed the cigar tube into his back with all the force she could muster. "Don't move. I have a gun and I know how to use it."

Eduard lifted both hands to shoulder height, palms outward, careful not to move suddenly. He hadn't allowed for his ghost to tote a gun and didn't care for the businesslike way it pressed against his back. "We can work this out. Don't do anything you'll regret."

"You seem sure I'll regret it."

The melodious voice reminded him of bells, and he itched to turn around and get a look at the owner. "Have you shot many people?" he asked.

"Only the ones who barge into my home while I'm out. You're remarkably well dressed for a burglar. Who are you?"

Her home? He decided against arguing for the moment. "My name is Eduard de Marigny."

He flinched as the gun barrel burrowed harder.

"Right, and I'm Princess Adrienne. I may be from Australia, but I know that de Marigny is the name of the Carramer royal family. You'll have to come up with a better alias because I've met Eduard."

This was news to him. Unable to resist, he glanced over his shoulder, catching a glimpse of shoulder-length ash-blond hair and a porcelain complexion. Cornflower eyes were trained on him as intensely as her weapon. A very attractive ghost, he judged. Her musical voice definitely held a hint of the Australian heritage she claimed, overlaid with something more European.

He sighed. "My name is Eduard Claude Philippe de Marigny, Marquis of Merrisand, currently with the rank of commander in the Carramer Royal Navy. I have identification in my shirt pocket if you'd care to examine it."

He heard her indrawn breath as if she recognized his titles. But the gun barrel didn't waver as she slid a slender hand around his chest and felt her way to his pocket. The lightly caressing touch made his heart pick up speed. He decided there were better ways to introduce himself to the young lady.

Reflexes and training allowed him to grasp her wrist, jerk her off balance, and spin her around in front of him so she fell into his arms. He tightened them around her, seeing that the weapon which dropped from her hand was only an old cigar tube of Prince Henry's. He had to give his ghost full marks for ingenuity.

He looked down at the woman in his arms. In close-up, her blond hair was sun-streaked and cascaded around her shoulders in soft waves, framing delicate features that wouldn't have been misplaced on a model.

"A most attractive ghost," he murmured.

She struggled in his grasp. "What are you talking about? Let me up."

He held tight, since it wasn't exactly a hardship. "First I want to make sure that you're human."

He hadn't intended to kiss her, but the temptation was too great. In his arms she felt as light as a feather, but she had her share of muscles, he noticed. Her shape and build suggested someone who took very good care of herself.

Her mouth was a shell-pink bow, curved now in

fury, and her eyes sparked a warning at him. He ignored it and lowered his lips to hers. She tasted of the baking he'd smelled when he walked in, yeasty, warm, thoroughly inviting.

She tasted so good that he took his time over the kiss, aware that at some point she gave up fighting him, and brought her arms around him. She probably thought she was stopping herself from falling, but that didn't explain the way her mouth opened so temptingly. If he'd been kissing her for real, he knew exactly how he would have responded to those parted lips.

But this wasn't the time. As it was, he had let the kiss go on far longer than was wise, the heat racing through him testifying to how much he had enjoyed it. Setting her upright and away from him took considerable self-restraint.

Looking confused, she backed away a little, but her cheeks glowed and her eyes glittered as if she had also enjoyed the experience more than she thought she should. "What did you do that for?"

"When I arrived, I thought the place was haunted. I had to make sure you aren't a ghost."

"You're crazy."

"And you're trespassing. Who are you, and what are you doing here?"

She made a choking sound. "*I'm* trespassing? You're the interloper. I own this place."

His intense gaze raked her, what he saw distracting him from the obvious foolishness of her claim. "You look familiar. Who are you?"

She'd been thinking the same about him. "Carissa Day, and this is my home."

She saw his memory return in a rush. "Good grief, it *is* you, Cris."

"Nobody has called me Cris since I was fifteen. Except…Eduard? It really is you."

He had changed, she saw. As a teenager, he had worn his dark chestnut hair longer. In the navy he had grown from a shy, slightly bookish teenager into a solidly built man who looked as if he could handle himself in most situations. He folded his arms over his chest, evidently enjoying her astonishment. "Told you so."

She had also changed, but she doubted if he saw as much progress as she did in him. When he'd last seen her, she had been long-legged and coltish, as if her limbs had outgrown her body. Her hair had been shorter and darker, and she'd worn glasses instead of the contacts she wore now.

Unwillingly reminded of the last time he had kissed her, all those years ago, she struggled to compose herself. "Of all the people who might have walked in here, you're the last person I expected to see."

"I don't know why," he observed. "Tiga Lodge has been in the family for a century. Prince Henry owned it until he died last year."

She felt a frown etch itself between her eyes. "That must be why it was on the market."

He took her arm. "You and I need to talk, Cris…Carissa."

"It's okay. Cris sounds good the way you say it." Like a homecoming, she thought.

Telling herself she was bemused by his sudden appearance, not by his kiss, she let him steer her back along the hall toward the kitchen. She saw his look register that the laundry had been removed from the line, and felt herself color, thinking of him seeing the lacy garments. She was glad she had moved them on the way in. Her days of hoping to attract Eduard's attention with her feminine wiles were long gone, although the way she felt now suggested otherwise. It was the aftermath of shock, nothing more, she reminded herself. Until a second ago, she had thought he was an intruder.

"Are your father and brother with you?" he asked.

She lowered her long lashes. "Dad died a year ago from a sudden heart attack."

"I'm sorry to hear that."

She inclined her head in silent acknowledgment.

"Is Jeffrey still in Australia?"

"Dad left the family home to him." She couldn't disguise the bitterness she'd felt when she'd found that out. No doubt Graeme Day had believed he was doing the right thing by specifying in his will that Jeffrey was to look after Carissa until she married. Embarrassed, Jeff had insisted on paying her half of the house's value in cash, but it hadn't assuaged her hurt. Or eased the sense of rootlessness that had plagued her all her life.

Their mother had died soon after she was born, and the family had lived in the Australian house for only a handful of years, so there was no reason for Carissa to think of it as home. But it was the only one she had. To have it bequeathed to her brother alone had hurt beyond measure. She had known her father had oldfashioned views about women, but had never dreamed he would do such a thing.

"Your accent doesn't sound as Australian as I remember," Eduard said, drawing her back to the present.

"I spent the last few years studying hotel management in Switzerland. After I graduated, I worked there for a while before being offered a job in Sydney."

Eduard took a seat at the huge kitchen table and his

palms skimmed the scrubbed pine surface. "Sitting here takes me back. My brother and I must have spent hours at this table, eating slabs of bread fresh from the oven, swearing the cook to secrecy so our parents wouldn't find out we'd been fraternizing with the staff."

Eduard had always been the more informal of the royal brothers, she recalled, unwillingly reminded of how she had once mistaken his friendliness for something more. She busied herself filling a kettle. "Do you still like your coffee black?"

He nodded. "You have a good memory."

She forebore telling him that she hadn't forgotten anything that had passed between them. Moments later she carried two cups of coffee to the table. Between them she placed a sliced tea cake. "I made it this morning."

He took a slice and bit into it. "No wonder I could smell baking when I walked in. This is good."

Her face twisted into a frown. "The agent selling this place told me the owner was away in the navy. Did he mean you?"

Eduard nodded. "The lodge originally belonged to my uncle, Prince Henry de Valmont."

"The agent mentioned the former owner's name. I knew de Valmont was a royal family name, but that's all. I wonder why the agent didn't tell me the house had been a royal lodge?"

"Probably because it still is."

She felt the color drain from her face and gripped the edge of the table so hard that her knuckles whitened. "Oh no."

"I'm sorry if that comes as a shock to you, Cris."

Her eyes brimmed and she blinked furiously. "You don't know the half of it."

"You'd better tell me the rest."

She drew a shuddering breath. "You didn't authorize an agent to sell the house discreetly for you, did you?" She was afraid she already knew the answer.

"I'm afraid not. Tiga Lodge is part of Carramer's national estate. I have the right to live here and use it as I see fit, but I hold the title in trust for my heirs. No one in the family would consider selling it."

He leaned forward. "Are you feeling okay?"

"Actually I'm not." She pushed her chair back so hard that it tumbled over, and ran from the room.

There was a maid's powder room down the hall, and he followed her to it, finding her kneeling over the pedestal, her shoulders heaving.

As a navy man, he'd dealt with his share of seasick crewmates, although he'd never suffered from the malady himself. He leaned over Carissa, stroking her hair and murmuring reassurance until the dreadful retching sound stopped. Then he helped her to stand, flushed the toilet and dipped a cloth into water to bathe her face. She felt as cold as ice and she trembled in his grasp. Her face was chalk-white as she sipped the glass of water he handed to her.

"All right now?" he asked.

She nodded. "Much better, thanks."

"Come back to the kitchen and finish your coffee. Unless you'd prefer to lie down. We can sort everything else out later."

"I would like to lie down, if you don't mind."

He helped her back to the room she had claimed, deciding to use another one for the time being. Something was wrong with her. Surely it wasn't only the shock of finding out that the lodge she thought she owned belonged to him? "Would you like me to send for a doctor? There's one in Tricot, about twenty minutes' drive away."

She stopped turning down the bedcovers and looked back at him. "I've already met him. He won't appreciate being dragged out here."

He gave a self-deprecating smile. "Rank has its privileges."

Carissa's face underwent a sea change. "I should have remembered. But there's no need, I'll be fine soon."

The coldness he heard in her tone puzzled him. He tried to think of a time when they were teenagers when he'd used his rank in some way she might have resented, but too much had happened today. "I'll let you get some rest," he said. "If you still feel ill later, I'm calling a doctor whether you want one or not."

She got into bed fully clothed, as if she felt too weary to undress. He debated whether to offer to help, then decided it wasn't such a good idea. Kissing her had already affected him more than was good for him. He had always been attracted to Carissa, even when she had been too young for him to make his feelings known except in a teasing way. Now that she was a woman, and a beautiful one at that, teasing hardly seemed appropriate. And he couldn't risk anything more.

Rank may have its privileges, but it also carried responsibilities. He had to be careful about indulging in romantic dalliances. The consequences could be dire, as he'd seen when his cousin, Michel, had been dubbed the playboy prince, his romances splashed across every newspaper in the country. And when Michel's sister, Princess Adrienne, had spent a night on a mountain alone with a man, they'd been forced to announce their engagement to avoid public censure. Eduard didn't want to put himself or any woman he cared about in such a position.

He frowned, thinking of his last disastrous attempt at romance. Lady Louise Mallon had been eminently suitable for him in every way, and Eduard had started to think something might come of their relationship.

The rest of his family would have been delighted, he knew, wondering what they would think if he told them she had become pregnant by another man, then tried to convince Eduard that the child was his. Her face had been a study when Eduard told her he could give her everything except children, which was why he had balked at proposing.

The real father of Louise's baby had come to Eduard and told him he wanted to marry her and raise the baby no matter who the father was. Eduard didn't intend to share the truth with a stranger. Prolonged exposure to toxic chemicals while helping to rescue the crew of a damaged ship had left Eduard unable to father children of his own. Apart from the royal physician, the only people who knew the truth were his immediate family.

He suspected he'd accepted the Australian assignment as much to get over the affair with Louise as to strengthen the ties between Carramer and Australia.

The last thing he needed was to create new problems for himself with Carissa. Bad enough that she was already living under his roof. That alone could cause difficulties. So he had two choices—get back into the chopper and go somewhere else, or arrange alternative accommodation for her as soon as possible.

Having just arrived, he didn't feel inclined to go somewhere less secluded, where his movements might be spied on by the paparazzi. In Tricot, the local people were used to the royal family's presence and respected their privacy. And no matter what Carissa believed, he owned the lodge. From the sound of things she had been the victim of a clever con artist. However sorry Eduard felt about that, she would have to be the one to leave.

When he looked in on her, she was asleep, her features at rest so she looked like a beautiful porcelain doll. She wasn't going to go quietly, he suspected, remembering what an emotional teenager she had been. If he'd had the slightest inkling that his intruder was Carissa, he would never have kissed her so impulsively. At least she behaved as if she was long over the crush she'd had on him when they were younger, but there was no point playing with fire.

As he unloaded the rest of his gear and provisions from the helicopter, he let his thoughts linger on the woman sleeping in his bed with one arm over her head and the other curved across her slim body. He'd been tempted to stay and watch her for the sheer pleasure of it, but he'd made himself move. She'd mistaken his attention for something stronger once. He wasn't going to make that mistake again.

He winced, remembering what a complete klutz he had been around women when he was in his teens. Carissa had been the only female with whom he could relax and be himself. Whether her Australian informality was the reason, or whether it was something about Carissa herself, he didn't know. But he had talked to her for hours as they took long walks along the beach at Chateau Valmont.

He had been stranded in the breach between school and university while Carissa was on vacation from the diplomatic high school. Already ahead of her age group, she had intrigued him with her intelligence and quick wit. Laughter had been their common bond and he'd thought she was as comfortable with their friendship as he was himself.

When Carissa threw herself into his arms and kissed him, telling him she was falling in love with him, he simply hadn't known how to react. He had treated her declaration as a joke. Not knowing what else to do, he had walked away, avoiding her for the rest of her vacation.

Before he left for university, he had tried to apologize and Carissa had accepted his apology stiffly, making him worry that her declaration of love hadn't been a joke to her. By the time he came home on vacation, her father had been posted back to Australia. Eduard hadn't heard from her again, so he'd had no further opportunity to make amends.

He knew he would respond differently if she threw herself at him now. She had turned into a beautiful, desirable woman. Holding her had felt better than anything Eduard had done in a long time.

Kissing her had felt better still. Unlike the last time, he knew exactly how to react. He was doing it now, just thinking about her. He would have preferred to send her on her way today, although he wasn't sure for whose benefit. By the time she woke up, it would be too late for her to go anywhere.

He carried the last of his gear inside, then went out and secured the chopper for the night. He was rated for night flying and could have flown Carissa wherever she wished to go, but he couldn't bring himself to eject her while she was so obviously unwell, assuming she had somewhere else to go.

Where she went wasn't his problem, he told himself. He hadn't conned her into buying the royal retreat. A few simple checks would have revealed the truth, then she wouldn't be in this fix. Why was she here anyway? She may have fallen in love with Carramer; foreigners frequently did. But lots of places were more accessible than Tiga Falls. The family had built the lodge precisely because of its location, to provide an ideal retreat from royal duty. What was Carissa retreating from?

He let out a long breath. Common sense dictated that he stop wondering and concern himself with seeing her on her way. But common sense had nothing to do with the instant, primitive way he responded to thoughts of her. He had a feeling that getting her out of his hair was going to be easier than getting her out of his mind.

Chapter Two

When Carissa awoke, she was surprised to find it was morning. Although she had slept well enough, she felt lethargic. Last night, Eduard had insisted she stay in bed and had brought her an omelet and a sliced Carramer peach. Impressive for a man who was accustomed to being waited on, she told him, using humor to disguise her reaction to him.

He had learned to cook in his spare time while at sea, he explained. While she ate, he had kept her company, but had refused to let her talk about the lodge, insisting that the problem could wait until morning when she felt better. She wondered if he would be so tolerant if he knew the real cause of her "flu."

She was violently ill almost as soon as she arose, and was glad that Eduard didn't see her undignified dash into the en suite bathroom. Why didn't she tell him she was pregnant? she wondered, as she returned to the bed to catch her breath.

The answer came straight away. She didn't want to

disappoint him. After all this time, she still cared what he thought of her. Fool, she lectured herself. How many times did he have to reject her before she accepted that he wasn't interested? If he were, he'd have answered at least some of the letters she wrote to him after returning to Australia. But he hadn't. After his stiff apology for hurting her feelings, she hadn't heard from him again.

She sipped a glass of tepid water, knowing she didn't regret the baby she was carrying. She had met Mark Lucas, a handsome, personable investment broker, through her brother, who was in the same field. She had been assistant manager of a boutique hotel. After she had learned that her father hadn't left her a share in the family home, she and Mark had already discussed moving to Carramer, and had set the wheels in motion. Mark had assured her he wanted the move as much as she did, but for different reasons, she knew now. According to her brother, Mark's business was struggling. He had probably thought moving to Carramer would give him a fresh start.

She and Mark had been seeing one another for six months before they had made love. Mark had wanted to long before, but she had preferred to wait. Then in the aftermath of her father's death, she had turned to Mark for comfort, too grief stricken to think of taking precautions. When she found out she was pregnant after only one night with Mark, she was so delighted she wondered if that had been her unconscious wish all along. A baby would give her the family she so longed for. Foolishly she had expected Mark to feel the same way.

Her fantasy had been shattered when she'd discovered he didn't want children. He'd been one of six brothers, and he didn't intend to struggle like his parents, he told her. When she informed him that she was expecting his child, he had offered her money to, as he put it, "solve the problem." She realized what he meant and had thrown the offer back at him and walked out.

Whatever her motive for getting pregnant, she wanted this baby with an intensity that astonished her. She linked her hands in front of herself in a protective gesture, although it was too early to feel any changes yet. Mark might think of the baby as a problem, but Carissa cherished the life growing within her because it meant having someone upon whom she could lavish all the love inside her at long last. She didn't expect Eduard to understand any more than Mark had done.

Finding the lodge had seemed like fate. She had paid the con man half the money Jeff had given her as her share of their father's house, keeping the rest for redecorating. The con man had told her she could move in right away, assuring her that her mortgage repayments wouldn't start until the lodge was earning an income. With a doctor available in Tricot to see her through her pregnancy, she had felt like the luckiest person in the world.

Lucky? She almost laughed out loud. If she'd suspected that Eduard really owned the lodge, she would have had nothing to do with it.

She shuddered, remembering how she had believed herself in love with him when she was a teenager. With the Australian Embassy located next door to Eduard's home in Perla, their paths often crossed socially. In the eighteen months she had lived in Carramer, they had become friends.

On Eduard's part, that's all it was, she understood

now. Perhaps her lack of family and roots, and her father's emotional distance, had made her susceptible to reading too much into the relationship, but she had believed that Eduard had shared her feelings.

Knowing he would soon be leaving for university, she had kissed him with all the passion in her soul. He had stood like a statue, his mouth cold against hers and his body stonily unresponsive. When she'd stammered out her feelings, he had dismissed them with unfeeling arrogance. She had wanted the ground to open up and swallow her. The stiff apology he made before he left had only made her feel more stupid and naive.

She pressed her hands to her cheeks, which burned as hotly as her memories. When he'd swept her into his arms yesterday, he must have been aware of her instinctive response. Was she destined always to make a fool of herself around him?

Her only consolation was that Eduard didn't seem to remember that teenage kiss. He had been the one to kiss her yesterday. She touched her fingers to her mouth, as if she could still feel the pressure of his lips against hers. He was no man of stone now. No statue could generate the heat inside her that his touch had done. She felt a resurgence of it now, just thinking about him.

Annoyed with herself, she drowned the feelings under a cool shower then dressed in a white shirt and olive cargo pants. Leaving her feet bare, she went to the kitchen to make toast, which was about all the breakfast she could face at present. From the plate and cup on the drainer, she saw that Eduard had already beaten her to it.

Later she tracked him down to the study she had looked forward to using as her own. She felt cheated at seeing him looking so at home behind what she'd thought of as her desk. Nor did she welcome the quick flutter in her stomach at the sight of him.

She placed the worthless sale contract on the desk in front of him. "I should have known this deal was too good to be true."

Eduard leafed through the papers, stopping to read a clause now and then. When he looked up, he said, "These are good, very good. But the royal family only uses one intermediary and it isn't…" he glanced at the name of the selling agent "…Dominic Hass. Where did you meet this man?"

She sighed. "I was staying at the Monarch Hotel in Tricot. He must have overheard me talking on my cell phone to my brother. I told Jeff that I was going to look at a property for sale out this way. After I hung up, Hass came up and asked my advice about where to take his mother sight-seeing. His mother! I must have *sucker* written on my forehead."

Eduard tilted the swivel chair backward, resting his fingertips on the desk for balance. "Don't blame yourself. People like Hass can be very convincing."

"He struck up a conversation. When I told him I planned to open a bed-and-breakfast place in the area, he told me he was the agent for a property that might interest me." She looked around her. "I should have smelled a rat when he didn't have a key. The lock was broken, probably by him. He said the keys had been lost."

This elicited a frown from Eduard. "That explains how he managed to gain entry. The lodge has never been up for sale."

She couldn't conceal her bitterness. "I know that now. Hass looked well-dressed and trustworthy." She might have been describing Mark, she thought with sudden insight. Or Eduard himself. She would definitely have to be more wary of good-looking men.

Eduard leaned across the desk. "How did he convince you of his credentials? I'm not rubbing it in, but the more you can recall about him, the greater the chance of the police catching him."

"He showed me glowing references from some of the people I remember from my father's time here, including you." She fished in her pocket and pulled out a business card. Hass's name mocked her from the glossy surface as she handed it to Eduard.

He studied the card thoughtfully. "The details are probably as phony as his references. Did he have an accent?"

"Vaguely British, I think, but difficult to pin down."

"He probably travels around the region, looking for new victims and staying a step ahead of local law. The local authorities may already have a file on him. He probably targeted you, as a foreigner, because..."

"Because I don't know any better than to buy up chunks of Carramer's national estate." She took a deep breath. "I'm not going to see my money back, am I?"

"Probably not."

She sank onto a chair in front of the desk. With most of her nest egg gone, she couldn't afford to remain in Carramer for long. Her brother would give her a home until the baby was born, but the thought of confessing her present plight to him didn't appeal at all.

"Still feeling unwell?" Eduard asked, watching her.

She lifted her head. "A little."

"You do look washed-out."

"Kind of you to say so." She let her ironic tone thank him for his encouragement.

His aristocratic eyebrows lifted. "I wasn't criticizing, merely stating a fact."

"Sometimes 'facts' can be damaging, whether you mean them to or not."

"Would you prefer me to lie to you?"

"I'd rather this whole mess hadn't happened." To her horror, she felt tears pool in her eyes. She blinked hard, but two droplets escaped down her cheeks.

Although she dashed them away furiously, Eduard noticed. He stood up, looking distressed. "Cris, please don't."

He had never been comfortable with emotions, she reminded herself, determined not to burden him with hers any longer. She got up. "I'll start packing right away."

Eduard stayed her with a sharp command. "Don't go, not like this. I'd like to help if I can."

Remembering how he had trampled on her feelings once before, she shook her head. "I got myself into this and I'll get myself out again. I don't need charity."

"I'm not offering any, but I have an idea that may help." He paused, then said, "Haven't you wondered why I have the title of marquis, theoretically outranking my older brother?"

Her confusion increased. "I assumed it's a Carramer tradition." But she sat down again.

Eduard laced his fingers together on the desk. "In a way, it is. The Merrisand title traditionally passes down my mother's line to the youngest child. One of her ancestors, also a youngest child, managed to offend a past ruler of Carramer and was given the title as an insult."

What did this have to do with her? Still, she couldn't resist asking, "Why was it an insult?"

"In Carramer mythology, Merrisand is a place that doesn't exist except in imagination, what you might call a fool's paradise."

She bristled. "I know I've been living in one since I got here, but I don't think..."

"I wasn't referring to you," he said before she could finish. "My forebear turned the title into an honorable one by setting up a charitable trust in that name. He built Merrisand Castle which still stands as a tourist attraction, the income going to the trust. With the title, I inherited responsibility for the trust. When Prince Henry left me the lodge, I decided to make it into a tourist facility to aid the trust, not unlike your plans for it."

"The difference being you own it, I don't."

He gave her a wry smile. "Did you own the hotels you worked in?"

She stared at him, perplexed. "Are you offering me a job?"

"You have the skills and experience to run such an establishment, more than I do, come to that. You could set the lodge up and operate it until I finalize my tour with the navy in the next few months."

"You have staff coming out of your ears."

Her turn of phrase provoked another smile. "Staff, yes. People accustomed to running palaces and royal tours. It's hardly comparable to looking after tourists."

"True." She quelled the expectancy rising inside her. Could this possibly answer her prayers? "What would I have to do?"

"Help me set up and run the best tourist facility in Carramer in aid of the Merrisand Trust."

"What happens after you leave the navy?"

"We can discuss that when the time comes."

By then she would be noticeably pregnant. Her original plan had been to work steadily on the refurbishing for as long as she could, then take the time she needed to have her baby and recover before opening the place to visitors. Eduard was hardly likely to want to wait that long. She found it hard to say, "Thank you, but I don't think so."

"Why? It's not as if you have competing offers."

She made a face. "You really should stop boosting my ego, or I'll end up with a swollen head."

"I didn't mean…"

"Let's face it, you don't really want me around. You're only offering me a job to ease your conscience, but there's no need. I'll be fine." She was probably flouting protocol by not letting him finish. She didn't care. She only wanted this over with. His job offer tempted her more than she wanted to admit, but her pregnancy made it impossible.

Overseeing the lodge for someone as demanding as Eduard would entail stress she didn't need right now. And soon her condition would begin to show. How long would Eduard want her on his payroll then? Better to leave with dignity while she still could.

"My conscience is clear," he surprised her by saying. "I didn't con you into buying a pig in a poke."

She hitched her fists onto her hips. "So you're saying I'm stupid?"

"How do you figure that?"

"Well, I must be, mustn't I? Any woman with half a brain would have seen through that smooth operator, instead of trusting him with every cent she had in the world."

This time she did break down, unable to stem the tears cascading down her cheeks. Eduard was at her side in an instant, his arms enfolding her as he murmured to her in the lilting Carramer tongue.

Twelve years had banished much of the language she'd picked up, but the comfort in his tone reached her, his consideration making her feel worse. She dragged in a lungful of air, trying to stop the sobs welling up from her depths.

"Don't fight it, let the tears come," he said in English. "You'll feel better afterward."

She didn't want to feel better. She didn't want to be in his arms, fighting a war with herself over whether to ask him to kiss her again. Hadn't she learned anything from her experience with her baby's father, and from the cold way Eduard himself had rejected her? Suddenly she didn't know if she was crying because of the lousy hand she'd been dealt, or because she knew Eduard wasn't for her.

Both were excuses to feel thoroughly miserable, she thought sniffing hard. Pregnancy must be playing havoc with her hormones to make her come apart so completely.

Eduard offered her a fine lawn handkerchief with his crest embroidered in one corner, a reminder if she needed one, of his status relative to hers. She blew her nose and dabbed at her streaming eyes. "I'm not usually this much of a wimp."

"Neither are you entirely well. Maybe we should have this discussion again when you're fully recovered."

He began to rub the small of her back. The circular movement of his hand against her back felt so comforting that she wanted to purr. All the more reason to put some distance between them. Why was she finding it so hard to do?

"Eduard," she began diffidently.

His face was buried in her hair. "Mmmm."

"You can let me go now. I'm all cried out."

"Maybe I don't want to let you go."

He had been ready enough to do so when she was a teenager. "You can't make me take the job," she said.

"Who said anything about the job? You feel fine right where you are."

Heaven help her, she agreed. After her father had died, and then Mark had rejected their child, she'd felt more lonely than she'd thought possible. She wasn't usually given to self-pity but the realization that she was officially an orphan had created a chasm inside her that seemed impossible to fill. Her father had been an only child, and hadn't heard from his parents in England in years. He had lost touch with her mother's family after she'd died. So, apart from her brother, Carissa had no close family. No wonder her desire for a child of her own had overwhelmed her common sense.

She told herself the surge of pleasure she felt in Eduard's arms was only because she was lonely. Unable to resist, she lifted her head and looked at him. He must have read the naked need in her gaze, because he bent his head and claimed her mouth, filling her with desire so wild it was like a bushfire tearing through her.

She tried ordering herself to relax. Hormones, only hormones, she told herself. She wasn't going to give any man the chance to treat her badly again, remember? So who was that woman answering his kiss with so much passion?

Her mind reeled as his tongue met hers in an unbelievably seductive dance. She placed her hands on his chest, thinking to push him away, but he trapped her hands against the fiery heat of his body, right where his heart pounded under her fingers. She could feel hers keeping time.

Heat flickered through her, making nonsense of her attempt to remain aloof. When had she been able to do any such thing around Eduard de Marigny? As a boy, he had enchanted her with his darkly handsome looks and challenging air of reserve. As a man he was even more handsome, but with a strength and self-assurance that had been missing from the boy. The result was breathtaking, literally.

"I can't do this," she said, all but suffocated by sensation.

"You're doing remarkably well," he murmured.

She persisted, pressing her palms against him to signal her seriousness. "Everything's moving too fast. First I thought the lodge was mine, now I find it's yours."

"No reason you can't be part of the package," he said.

"No!" This time she made sure he understood her rejection of this notion.

He created a heartbeat of space between them and looked down at her, his gaze puzzled. "What's the matter, Cris? To me, this feels pretty right."

"You could have fooled me." She couldn't keep the bitterness out of her voice.

A frown etched a deep V in his forehead. "What do you mean?"

She hadn't intended to remind him, but she was committed now. "When I was fifteen, I kissed you and you treated me as if I'd just crawled out from under a rock."

He released her. "I was only eighteen myself. I didn't have much skill at dealing with women."

And now he did. The thought wasn't as comforting as she knew he meant it to be. A wave of something very like jealousy overcame her. Her voice dropped to a whisper. "I thought you were attracted to me."

Eduard let out a long breath. "I was."

She hadn't expected this. "Then why did you go out of your way to avoid me until you left for university?"

"I didn't know any other way to handle a lovestruck fifteen-year-old. I obviously couldn't encourage your attention."

"Because I'm not royal like you?"

He crooked a finger under her chin and tilted her face up. "Because you were still a child."

She wasn't a child any longer, and his closeness threatened to overwhelm her defenses. "Just as well it was only a crush. I got over it."

"Did you, Cris?"

"Of course." The shakiness in her voice made the lie obvious.

Evidently not to Eduard. "Then all I can say is I'm sorry. I thought you wanted me to kiss you."

If he only knew. "People change," she said with a lightness that didn't quite come off.

"I haven't. Not where my affection for you is concerned."

"Don't, Eduard, please." To find that he had cared about her after all was almost more than she could bear.

"Is there someone in your life?"

"Yes." She didn't tell him the someone was her unborn child.

"I see." He turned away and paced to the window. "Is he planning to join you here?"

"We haven't worked out the details."

Eduard spun around. "Then why not stay and manage the lodge? There's a caretaker's cottage that could be made into a separate home.''

Dare she say yes? She knew he meant that she and the man he believed she was involved with could use the caretaker's cottage, while she helped him get the lodge ready to open. Did it matter if the other person in her life turned out to be a baby? Of course it did, she accepted. Look at the damage one misunderstanding between them had done. Who knew what harm could come of starting out with another?

''Don't give me your answer yet,'' he urged before she could say anything. ''I'd like to look around the estate first, get a feel for what might be done with it. Will you stay while we work up a plan of action?''

The pleasure shafting through her was out of all proportion to his suggestion. But it meant she could stay for a few more days. And she would be gone before he found out about the baby, so he need never feel disappointed in her. Now she knew that he *had* been attracted to her, she didn't think she could cope with that.

''I'll stay. Once we report what happened with the con man, I'll need to be available for the police to interview me,'' she said, knowing the excuse sounded lame. She could be interviewed equally well at the hotel in Tricot.

''You should.'' He matched the seriousness of her tone.

She laughed nervously. ''You said they would want to.''

''And your con man might have left the country by now.''

His comment plunged her into gloom, emphasizing that she stayed by Eduard's grace and favor. The thought took some of the gloss off the idea. She was tempted to change her mind. Playing house in what she had thought of as her home only postponed the inevitable. She still had to make a life for herself and the baby. With only the money she had set aside to redecorate the lodge, it wouldn't be easy. Why not face it now and get it over with?

Her expression must have telegraphed her intention, because Eduard said, "I mean to put our arrangement on a business footing, starting now."

"What?"

"I intend to pay you a salary while you're assisting me."

She studied him suspiciously. "You wouldn't be trying to make up for my losses, would you, your lordship?"

He lifted his hands, flattening his palms. "When we were younger, you called me that when you thought I was getting high and mighty. Offering to pay you isn't in that class." He shifted uncomfortably. "Putting you on my staff would serve to defuse any gossip that might arise out of your presence here."

"It's okay for you to have a female under your roof, as long as she's a servant?" She knew she sounded angry and couldn't make herself care. She felt as if she was fifteen again, being put in her place. "I think it's best if I leave now."

He touched her arm. "Cris, I didn't ask to be royal. Things are simpler this way, trust me."

His statement took the wind out of her sails. "I know, and I shouldn't overreact. But if I'm to be paid for working for you, I want to do a real job."

He looked relieved. "I can turn into a slave driver

if you prefer. Some of the men under my command already think of me as one.''

''I don't doubt it.'' She had seen firsthand how autocratic he could be when he wanted. Catching sight of the twinkle in his dark gaze, she realized he was joking.

''Do we have a deal?''

Her sigh gusted out. She had known what she would say the moment he offered her the job. She wanted to stay with him. ''Deal.''

He smiled and her heart turned over. ''I'll brush up on my slave-driving skills just for you.''

He wouldn't have to, she knew. This was familiar territory. Challenged by his offer, her mind was already racing ahead as she ticked off requirements on her fingers. ''We'll need a business and financial plan for the lodge. That would be your department.'' She took a breath. ''As soon as the financials and decorating theme are in place, I can draw up a schedule for tradespeople to do the work, and a program for hiring and training staff, starting with a house manager, catering manager, executive housekeeper and front office staff.''

He looked slightly bemused. ''Agreed. Right after you put your feet up for a while.''

Shock jolted through her. Had he guessed her secret already? ''Excuse me?''

''You're still recovering from the flu. No feudal lord worth his salt makes his serfs work when they're ill. Serfs are expensive to replace,'' he added when she shot him a quizzical look.

''You're the boss,'' she admitted.

His gaze glimmered with satisfaction. ''Now we're getting somewhere.''

Chapter Three

Despite his promise to be a slave driver, Carissa could hardly complain that Eduard was too hard on her in the days that followed. His presence made it easier for her to give her statement to the police, although it couldn't have been every day that someone tried to buy a royal lodge. They promised to do everything they could to catch the con man, mainly because of Eduard's involvement, she assumed. The officers held out little hope of catching up with Mr. Hass, or whatever his real name was. Like Eduard, they believed he had probably left Carramer as soon as he had his hands on her money.

Unable to do anything more for the moment, she threw herself into the challenge of recreating the lodge as a tourist venture. Eduard was enthusiastic about her ideas for turning the lodge into an environmentally friendly place to stay, adding suggestions she had discarded as being beyond her limited budget.

She was amazed that someone with his background,

accustomed to having servants to do his bidding, could be so practical. He crawled around loft spaces, had her hold a tape measure while he measured rooms and showed a knack for seeing not what was, but what could be. He credited the navy with making him so efficient, but privately she thought that Eduard gave his own resourcefulness too little credit.

She immersed herself in lists. Since she wasn't familiar with the local tradespeople, she decided to search out an agency to do the actual hiring, based on the skills the lodge would need.

Juggling existing and potential numbers of rooms and occupancy rates, she soon had lists of furnishings and supplies that would have been impossible on her limited budget. Eduard's involvement gave her the freedom to let her head go. If a nagging voice warned her against getting too involved, she chose to ignore it, along with the fear that she was living in her own version of a fool's paradise.

"What do you think of converting the old stables into luxury accommodation to encourage groups to hold conferences here?" she asked as they worked outside in the brilliant morning sunshine.

She tried not to be distracted by the way the sunlight burnished his hair, and turned his skin to gold. He managed to look regal in a cream open-necked shirt and stone-washed jeans, a pair of well-worn running shoes on his feet. Now that she knew he *had* been interested in her when they were younger, she could no longer use antipathy as a barrier against his attractiveness.

How would things have worked out if he had kissed her back, instead of avoiding her? Probably exactly the same, she thought with an inward sigh. Her age had made anything else impossible. Her father would still have been posted back to Australia, and Eduard would have continued his royal life without her. Why hadn't he married by now? He was a long way from the throne of Carramer, but he would be expected to produce his share of heirs to the titles he had inherited.

He gave a low whistle. "You didn't hear a word I said, did you?"

She pulled her attention back to the present, aware that wool-gathering was a common side effect of pregnancy, although she hadn't experienced any difficulty keeping her mind on a task before Eduard arrived. "I...uh...no, I didn't."

"Thought so." He stood up and reached for her hand, urging her to her feet. "We need some exercise. You haven't visited Tiga Falls yet, have you?"

She shook her head. "I've heard it's beautiful, but I wasn't sure how to get there."

He gestured airily. "Take a note, Ms. Day. Hiking trails to be marked out, and a map printed with estimated walking times and degrees of difficulty created."

She playfully started to write, but he snatched the file out of her hands and tossed it onto a picnic table. "We can't have all work and no play turning you into...no, you could never be dull, could you?"

She colored under his searching gaze. "You used to think I was."

"You were far from dull," he said softly. "I envied your exuberance. You were always full of life and fun."

"I didn't think you noticed."

"I noticed all right. But I was too unsure of myself to say anything. Around you, I felt like a stack of books with legs."

She laughed, remembering how single-mindedly he had tackled his studies with his tutors. "You were the keenest student I'd ever met."

"Goes with the territory," he said, sobering. "My father and Uncle Henry used to impress on Mathiaz and me that studying hard was a royal duty. Even when we played sport, we had to excel at it, or it wasn't worth doing."

"Which explains why you and Mathiaz creamed Jeff and me on the tennis court so often."

"We had lessons from professionals as soon as we were old enough to hold a racket."

"Be honest. You were also talented." While at university, he had represented Carramer at international level, she recalled. At seventeen, she had gone to see him play at the world championships in Melbourne without letting him know she was there. "Do you still play?"

"Only socially since I joined the navy. Flying's my sport these days."

He had shown her his helicopter soon after he arrived, offering to take her for a ride. To Carissa's nervous eye, the plastic bubble and flexible rotors looked too fragile to entrust with her life, so she had opted for a rain check. He hadn't teased her about her nervousness, but had assured her the offer was always open.

He went into the lodge and emerged with a small day pack. "Should I take anything?" she asked.

He shrugged the pack onto his broad shoulders. "I've put springwater, crackers and fruit in here, in case we get hungry on the way."

She managed to smile. He didn't know that she was always hungry lately, her rebellious stomach giving her little peace. Fortunately, Eduard blamed her erratic appetite on the aftermath of the flu and didn't ask awkward questions. She wasn't sure how long this could go on and knew she would have to make plans to leave the lodge soon. She should probably have left already. The salary Eduard was paying her, generous though it was, wouldn't make much of a dent in what she'd lost.

Who was she kidding? The salary wasn't half as appealing as the man paying it. She had thought she was over her infatuation with Eduard de Marigny. A week under the same roof with him was all it had taken to show her how easily her feelings could be reawakened.

Not that she was about to let that happen. All she wanted was to leave with her secret intact and start again somewhere else. If Mark Lucas hadn't been enough to convince her of the folly of trusting anyone, her experience with the con man had convinced her that she was better off taking care of herself. Somehow she would make a life for herself and her child without depending on a man, not even the dashing marquis.

In this frame of mind, she accompanied Eduard into the rain forest. He must have followed a map in his mind, because she couldn't see any difference between the way he went and any one of a dozen other openings between the trees. She was glad she hadn't tackled this walk without a guide.

"You'll have to mark the trail, unless you plan on taking every visitor to the falls personally," she said, catching up with him. After forty minutes of steady hiking he was still breathing easily, in contrast to the panting that passed for breath with her.

He noticed and slowed down. "I've done this trip so many times, I forget that others haven't."

"Is it much farther?"

"We'll take a break at the next clearing."

Ten minutes' walk brought them to a spectacular grove of painted eucalyptus and golden-stemmed bamboos. Eduard dropped his pack and propped himself against a fragrant allspice tree. She was happy to settle on a fallen log and regain her breath. Gratefully she opened the bottle of water he handed her and drank deeply. "This is lovely."

He passed her a package of crackers and a succulent peach, and she nibbled cautiously. When her stomach didn't rebel, she ate with more enthusiasm. What was it about fresh air that made food taste so delicious?

She glanced at him from under lowered lashes, almost groaning as she saw him bite into a peach, the juice trickling down the slight cleft in his chin until he wiped it away with the back of his hand. With his shirt half-unbuttoned for coolness, he looked less regal, more primitive. Seduction personified.

At a rustling sound in the bushes, she tensed and would have sprung to her feet, but Eduard held up a hand. "Sun deer," he whispered. "Over to your right."

She held still as a beautiful dappled creature emerged from the forest, paused for a moment on slender legs, ears erect and twitching, before bounding away among the trees. The sun deer was the faunal emblem of Carramer. She sighed happily. "I've heard of them, but that's the first one I've ever seen."

"They're increasingly rare. Some people never see one."

"Have you come across them here before?"

He nodded. "It's always a buzz."

He gave her a hand up, his touch sending powerful waves of sensation along her arm all the way to her heart. The magic of the rain forest enveloped her, undermining her need to stay uninvolved. The desire to have him take her in his arms was so strong that if she had known which direction to take back to the lodge, she would have headed there.

Eduard's expression was unreadable. She couldn't tell whether he was affected by the moment because he shouldered his pack and continued along the barely visible trail without comment.

The valley snaked through dense rain forest, bamboo groves and fern-covered hillsides. African tulip trees added splashes of orange. Now and again she glimpsed a native peacock and flocks of brightly colored Ramer parrots, but saw no more of the exquisite sun deer.

She heard the falls before she saw them. At first she didn't recognize the roaring sound, but as they came closer, the air became charged with fine mist. "Tiga Falls is up ahead," Eduard said.

He left the pack beside an allspice tree and took her hand to guide her along the slippery path leading to the waterfall. Suddenly she was confronted by a towering wall of rock down which crystalline water poured in an endless, shimmering torrent. Wild ginger grew on the path and ferns clung to the rock wall. Carissa didn't think she had ever seen anything more spectacular. The number of visitors who came here would have to be kept small, and they would have to be accompanied by a guide for their own safety and to protect this pristine environment, she thought.

She stood beside Eduard, her hand in his, lost in wonder until he said, "Traditionally, on your first visit, you're supposed to walk behind the falls to pay your respects to the Mayat spirits living in the cave."

She looked at him in surprise. "There's a cave behind the falls? I'd love to see it!"

The Mayat were the earliest known inhabitants of Carramer, reaching the islands by sea from the Philippines and Indonesia two thousand years before. Fragments of their jade work were still being unearthed in remote parts of the kingdom.

Most prized were the fingernail-sized charms called Mayati that had been exchanged as tokens of respect on special occasions. Carissa's father had given her a fern-shaped one as a birthday present and she still wore it occasionally.

Water misted her face as she approached the falls. Her feet almost went from under her, and Eduard's arm tightened around her waist. She was grateful for the support, but less certain of the dizzying sensation rocketing through her. If there had been a safe way to extricate herself, she would have, but negotiating the slick rocks without his help was courting disaster.

She saw the cave a moment later, like a yawning black mouth screened by crashing water. The surrounding rock was covered with ferns and flowering impatiens. Inside, she could imagine, it would be dripping wet and cool.

"What are you supposed to do once you get inside?" she shouted over the water's roar.

"This."

Before she had time to marshal her defenses, he had pulled her against him. She must look a sight, she thought. Eduard didn't seem to mind. Like hers, his hair and clothes were plastered to him with the spray. The damp clothes outlined his masculine contours as dramatically as if he'd been naked. Had the mist revealed her to him so completely? She caught her breath.

Her senses sharpened, swamping her with the scent

of ginger, the crisp mineral taste of the water, the slickness of skin meeting skin and the provocation of his firm mouth homing in on hers. Her whirling mind tried to grasp the reasons why this was a bad idea, but her thoughts cartwheeled away into pure desire and she tilted her head back.

Then she forced her eyes open. Soon she would be gone and Eduard's kisses would be a memory. Why not imprint this moment in her mind to relive when she was on her own again?

In the eerie light of the rain forest, his eyes looked like twin coals, burning with a fire that threatened to consume her. But he didn't take her willing mouth. Instead he planted a series of kisses from her forehead down her face to her throat. When he lifted his head, she felt her knees buckle.

He led her back from the seething water to a fallen log where she collapsed like a marionette whose strings have been cut. She felt as if every nerve had been short-circuited. "What did you do to me?" she demanded.

"Not me, the Mayat spirits. When the Kiss of Greeting is performed inside the cave, the Mayat are said to draw energy out of the participants to regenerate themselves. Some people don't feel a thing. Others swear they've been struck by lightning. I've been here many times without being affected, and I've never heard of anything happening outside the cave before."

"So they stock up on our energy, and we're left feeling as if we've wrestled ten rounds with a live gorilla."

He chuckled. "They do give something back." He hesitated, as if reluctant to tell her the rest.

She was too intrigued to give up. "Come on, what's the trade-off? Perfect hair? Invisibility?"

"Love."

She was glad of the fallen log beneath her, knowing her limbs would have given way at the sound of the single, softly spoken word. "How?"

"Some say the effect lets you reclaim a lost love, others that it lets you find the love you seek." He looked uncomfortable. "Don't worry, it's only a legend. You probably think you felt something because you're not fully recovered yet."

"Probably," she agreed, but privately doubted it. A more likely explanation was Eduard's own effect on her. He didn't look in the least affected, she noticed, her anger rising. How could she feel so shaken, while he looked as if he'd done no more than admire the scenery?

Obviously, in spite of his assurance, he didn't feel the same way about her as she felt about him. He might have been attracted to her when they were younger, but he had evidently outgrown the infatuation more successfully than she had.

She struggled to her feet, shrugging off the hand he put out to assist her. "I'm fine, thanks. You're probably right, there was no energy-zapping effect. I imagined the whole thing." Tell herself often enough, and she might start believing it.

He regarded her through narrowed eyes. "You're angry."

Of course she was angry. She'd marched through a rain forest, been soaked by a waterfall and left punch-drunk by a bunch of two-thousand-year-old spirits. And Eduard had felt nothing. "I'm not angry, just tired," she insisted.

"You haven't enjoyed yourself today?"

She couldn't tell him that she had enjoyed herself entirely too much. The bush walk was extraordinary. She had rarely felt so enchanted by an experience, and would sell her soul for a repeat.

Not the kiss. She didn't need the kiss, or its devastating after-effects, she told herself. But she had fallen in love with the rain forest, the waterfall with its mythical inhabitants and the magical sun deer. "I did enjoy myself," she admitted. "You're probably right, I'm not fully recovered yet." Nor would she be for another six months, but she couldn't very well tell him that.

"You will come back here."

His quiet assurance startled her and she lifted her head. "How can you be sure?" Especially when she wasn't.

"Once the Mayat have touched you, you're forever drawn to this spot."

"Another legend?"

"A promise." He bent toward her and skimmed her damp hairline with his lips, provoking a shiver. "I should warn you, the Mayat have a way of getting what they want."

They were the only ones, she thought unhappily. "Not this time."

"We'll see."

She watched him hook the pack over his shoulder. What was it about Eduard that reduced her from a sensible, capable woman to a quivering mess? She didn't believe for a minute that spirits were to blame. More likely her own foolish expectations where he was concerned. Expectations he clearly didn't share.

She told herself she was better off facing the truth. Without this experience, she might start imagining a future with Eduard that could never happen. Better to accept reality, and go on.

She had gone on once, she could do it again. This time she was older and wiser. All right older. If she had been wiser, she wouldn't have agreed to work for Eduard, far less accompany him to such a magical place as Tiga Falls. She had convinced herself that she could handle her feelings for Eduard, just as she had convinced herself that Mark Lucas wanted a baby as much as she did. How wrong could one woman be?

She walked with Eduard in thoughtful silence, letting the peace of the rain forest soothe her. The return seemed shorter than the outward leg. ''That's because you're on the way home,'' he said when she said so.

If only that were true. She had enjoyed thinking of the lodge as home, and she was going to miss it. She'd never felt as if she had a real home, and the terms of her father's will had excluded her from their house in Sydney.

She squared her shoulders, refusing to give in to self-pity. Working for Eduard, she would save as much as she could. Then she would find a home for herself and her child somehow. It might not be as special as the lodge, but this time she would make sure no one could take it away from them.

Chapter Four

Eduard turned and offered her a hand to help her negotiate the steep staircase leading to the attic. His grip felt warm and firm. He hadn't touched her since they returned from the falls two days ago, and she had missed the contact.

Not that he had been distant with her. After she'd inventoried the existing furnishings in the lodge and written out recommendations for improvements, he had accepted them without amendment, praising her efficiency. Outside working hours, they took turns making coffee and meals, then sat up late discussing plans for the lodge. She had no reason to be haunted by the feel of his lips against hers and his arms around her, but she was.

She was probably homesick, she told herself, although she hadn't missed Australia while she was working in Switzerland. And she had always been self-sufficient, forced into it at an early age by her father's career.

Very well, then. She was on the rebound from Mark and vulnerable to a handsome face and a winning smile. Eduard possessed both. She didn't have to let them affect her.

So why was she breathing so hard by the time she joined him in the attic?

He made a face, "You're out of shape, Cris."

She pulled back, unwilling to share the real reason with him. "You didn't tell me how steep the climb would be." She had intended to explore the attic before he'd arrived, but the weather had been so enticing that she had preferred working in the garden, and hadn't gotten around to coming up here until now.

She looked around. The ceiling sloped away to dormer windows on both sides, flooding the area with natural light. When she looked out, she could see for miles. There was plenty of headroom, too. Tall as he was, Eduard could stand upright easily.

"Properly decorated, and with a less-steep access, this would make a fantastic guest suite," she said.

His expression became nostalgic. "It made a pretty fantastic playroom, too. Until I was nine or ten, our family spent most of our vacations at the lodge. On rainy days, Josquin, Mathiaz and I would climb up here, and pretend the attic was a fort or an army encampment."

She had no trouble imagining the jumble of cabin trunks and furniture shrouded with dust sheets as hills and valleys, or the walls of a fort. Or picturing a young Eduard guarding his territory ferociously against his brother and cousin, both older than himself.

"Who won?"

He gave her a shrewd glance. "Mostly me and my

army. At least the one in my head. Josquin was a great fighter, and Mathiaz was the master strategist.''

She draped an arm over a dust-covered easel. ''So how come you won?''

He gave a lopsided grin. ''I made up the rules.''

''Wasn't that a bit devious?''

''I spelled them out beforehand. It wasn't my fault if they couldn't remember all the fine details.''

''You could, because you invented them.'' She paused thoughtfully. ''Do you apply the same tactics in the military?''

He crouched down and opened a battered leather trunk. ''When I have to.''

Eduard would always make his own rules, she decided. ''I heard about the rescue at sea,'' she said softly.

He kept his attention on the trunk. ''Oh, that.''

If she'd had any sense she would have heeded his offhand tone and changed the subject, but she might never have another chance to ask him about his role in the adventure that had been in all the papers and on television eighteen months before.

''From what I saw, you were quite a hero.''

He didn't look at her as he rummaged through the old photographs in the chest. ''Hardly a hero. More a case of being in the wrong place at the wrong time.''

''Not according to the crew of the cargo ship you fished out of a sea boiling with toxic chemicals. For them, you were in exactly the right place.''

He gave a slight shrug. ''I'm navy. It's part of my job.''

She remembered a comment made by a TV presenter. ''You were told if you went in, you'd be exposed to the chemicals, too. Yet you went anyway. You can't tell me that's part of your job. Another case of playing by your own rules?''

This time he looked at her. ''Sometimes there's nothing else you can do.'' He held up a fistful of photographs. ''Some of these might be useful as decorations for the lodge.''

Subject closed, she heard. She accepted the pictures which were mostly of the lodge and surroundings taken over several decades. She looked at them, but her mind was still on the scene she'd watched unfold on Swiss television. As soon as she'd heard that Eduard was involved in the rescue, she'd been unable to tear her eyes away.

A gale had been raging the night two cargo vessels had collided in the China Sea. The ship carrying the chemicals had careened wildly after the collision, hastening the spill from a breach in its hull. At times, she remembered, the ship had nearly keeled over as waves swamped the crew members waiting on the deck for rescue, washing many into the heaving water.

Eduard should have been in the relative safety of the captain's seat but had volunteered to be the rescue swimmer, swinging down on a cable to pick up the injured in the water. She had lost count of the times he'd been lowered into the swell and plucked another person to safety. She hadn't released a whole breath until he returned to the helicopter for the final time, and it had headed for the mainland.

She'd looked in vain for Eduard to be interviewed but she didn't catch so much as a glimpse of his face, although she had read later that he'd refused a medal for his part in the rescue. There were plenty of followup stories with the survivors, but from Eduard, no comment. He wasn't about to give her one now, she saw, disappointed. She wanted to tell him how much she admired what he had done, but he obviously didn't welcome any more discussion.

Fanning the photographs out in her hand, she said, "Here's one of you with your brother and Prince Josquin." With them was a young girl she didn't recognize.

"That picture must be over twenty years old. Josquin and Mathiaz were about eleven and I was nine or ten there." Eduard came up behind her to take a closer look at the photo, and his breath whispered across the back of her neck, sending messages of response down her spine.

The urge to lean against him was surprisingly hard to resist. She resisted anyway, as she had been resisting his nearness since he'd kissed her so potently at the falls.

The taste of his mouth, the skim of his fingers over her heated skin, the excitement building inside her, all were imprinted on her consciousness, to be relived as she lay in bed at night.

In dreams, not in reality. She was old enough now to know where her future lay—with her baby, not with a man who had a kingdom at his feet, and didn't need a pregnant foreigner in his life.

What was she doing here? As soon as she'd learned the truth about the lodge's owner, she should have packed and left. Carramer had a thriving tourism industry. With her training, she could support herself in any number of jobs.

The truth loomed as clearly as the photo in her hand. Against all logic, she wanted to work with Eduard. Perhaps she was still recovering from Mark's rejection of her and their child, but Eduard made her feel whole again. That he also made her feel desirable, she refused to explore. For now, he was good for her. Provided she kept her feelings in check, she would be fine.

After the visit to the falls, she had tried to stop herself getting too close to him, keeping her manner businesslike. But he was hard to resist. Even when they discussed color schemes and furniture arrangements, she found her thoughts straying into dangerous territory. In the cloistered atmosphere of the attic, her vow was almost painfully hard to keep.

She dragged in a breath to center herself, and focused on the picture, which she saw had been taken at Tiga Falls. The children must have been in the cave because their hair was slick with water and their clothes clung to them. Even then Eduard had been tall for his age and she could see in his lean features the promise of the man leaning over her shoulder. She swallowed hard.

"Who is the little girl?"

"She isn't a little girl any more," he said, an edge in his voice. "She's Louise Mallon, the daughter of the Archbishop of Carramer. As children, we saw quite a bit of one another. For a time, we were engaged to be married."

A sharp sense of anguish stabbed through Carissa. "I didn't know you were getting married."

"Past tense," he said gruffly. "It didn't work out."

Why not? she wanted to ask, but kept the question to herself. As a child, Louise Mallon had shown the promise of great beauty. And she was obviously the adventurous type, judging by this photo. She was as saturated as the royal cousins. "I'm sorry," she said, not sure how honestly.

"It's better to find out before, rather than after marriage,'' he said dismissively. He closed his hand around hers to steady the photo which trembled in her grasp.

The curl of his fingers around hers threatened to undermine her resolve. She told herself that lots of people touched hands. They even kissed one another. She didn't have to let it mean more than friendship.

Standing on the riverbank behind the children was a stern-looking man with ramrod-straight posture. A younger couple was with him. ''Your parents and Prince Henry?'' she said, freeing her hand to touch the figures. She had never met the old prince, but it wasn't hard to guess who such a stern-looking man had to be. When Eduard nodded, she asked, ''Where are your mother and father now?''

''Living in Paris. Father has been Carramer's ambassador to France for the last three years.''

''I wish I'd known they were so close by when I was in Switzerland. I could have contacted them. They were very kind to Jeff and me.''

''Mother would have liked to hear from you. From her calls and letters, she adores Paris, but she misses Carramer.''

''I know how she feels.''

''You?''

She knelt beside the trunk and replaced the bundle of photos. ''Your kingdom was the only place where I truly felt at home.''

''Yet you never wrote, never came back, not even for a vacation.''

Had he wanted her to? She shot him a look of surprise. ''For the first few months after we returned to Australia, I wrote every few weeks. You never replied, so I stopped writing.''

She didn't add that she hadn't stopped hurting from

the slight for a long time, or wishing that she hadn't thrown herself at him so recklessly. She had been torn between being glad of the ocean separating them, and wishing she could transport herself back to Carramer to be closer to him.

He took her hands and helped her to her feet, but didn't release her hands. ''I swear I never received any of your letters.''

Being held at arm's length was playing havoc with her vow of non-involvement. She seized on this new puzzle as a distraction. ''Then what happened to them?''

His hold tightened as his tone became earnest. ''A glitch in the postal service between Australia and here? I don't know. You must know I wouldn't just ignore them.''

''Dad,'' she said in sudden understanding.

Eduard looked puzzled. ''You think your father intercepted your letters?''

''He must have done.'' All these years she had believed Eduard didn't want anything more to do with her. To a fifteen-year-old in the throes of first love, the belief had devastated her. Now she was sure she had the answer. Overhearing Jeff teasing her about her crush on Eduard, her father had been furious. Only her sworn assurance that the marquis had done nothing to encourage her romantic feelings for him mollified her father. It wasn't a big step to imagine him destroying her letters for what he thought was her own good.

Hadn't he told her to stop mooning around and pull herself together?

Which was what she had done, making a success of her life and career, until her father died and she became pregnant by Mark. Was she fated always to be attracted to the wrong men? She pulled her hands free and began to tug dustcovers off some of the furniture around them.

Eduard dragged one of the covers out of her hands and threw it aside. "You do believe that I wouldn't ignore your letters?"

"At the time, I didn't know what to believe. Now?" She let her shoulders rise and fall eloquently. Telling him what she suspected would be far too revealing, so she said, "As you say, postal systems aren't infallible. It was a long time ago. I didn't die of disappointment." Did *almost* count?

"I would never deliberately hurt you, Cris."

He had already done so once, and was in danger of doing it again, but the problem was hers, she accepted. "I know," she said, trying to make her tone light. "It's probably just as well you didn't get the letters, when I think of the teenage nonsense I used to write."

"You could never write nonsense. I remember the prize you won for creative writing when you were at diplomatic school here. I read your story and enjoyed it."

She was surprised and flattered that he remembered. In her reading, she had come across one of the Mayat legends and adapted it as a contemporary love story between two teenagers from different worlds, fuelled no doubt, by her powerful feelings for Eduard. The story had been published by the *Valmont News* as part of her prize.

She felt warmth travel up her neck into her face. "I didn't know you'd seen it."

He nudged the dust sheet with his toe. "I may not have known how to respond to you back then, but it didn't mean I was unaware of you."

He spoke so softly that she regarded him in astonishment. She believed him when he blamed his coolness toward her years ago on inexperience. But that didn't mean she could afford to accept that things could be different between them now. There was still her pregnancy to consider. Eduard was unlikely to be attracted to her once he knew she carried another man's child, and she didn't think she could bear dealing with his rejection a second time.

"We all have to grow up sometime," she said with forced flippancy, and turned to the item she had uncovered. It was an ornately carved rocking chair, and she ran a hand appreciatively over the intricate surface. "This would look lovely in the living room downstairs. I wonder why it was consigned to the attic?"

"A lot of these pieces came from the old nursery," he explained. "When the room was no longer needed for that purpose, it was converted into a games room."

She knew which room he meant, having seen a billiard table there on one of her first explorations of the house. "All the same, it's a lovely piece of furniture. It's a shame to hide it away."

She sat down experimentally, smiling as she started the chair gently rocking. "I'll bet this chair has rocked many a royal baby to sleep." Perhaps Eduard himself. The chair looked as if it had been in the family long enough.

She had a fleeting glimpse of herself rocking her baby in the chair, and had to struggle to dismiss it from her mind. She stood up, narrowly avoiding stepping on a small foot. She bent and picked up the doll that had been lying beneath the chair.

The doll, a baby, had what looked like an original human hair wig, blond and covered by a crocheted bonnet. Her eyes were blue glass, opening and closing when Carissa tilted the doll back. She was dressed in a rust-colored challis coat over a white batiste gown. "She's beautiful," Carissa said. "She looks very old."

"She probably is," Eduard agreed. "We have old photographs showing the doll in the nursery at Merrisand Castle when my mother was a girl, so it could have belonged to her. Someone told me her name was Rosamond, but don't quote me on that. As a boy I was more into bows and arrows than dolls."

"Rosamond suits her." Carissa touched a finger to the doll's delicate hands. Something caught inside her and she realized she was cradling the doll as she would a real baby. Embarrassed, she placed it carefully on the seat of the rocking chair. "I don't suppose you'd consider using her in your decorating scheme?"

Eduard didn't seem to have noticed her response to the doll. He gave a gruff laugh. "She doesn't exactly fit the image of an eco-tourist establishment."

"But she does create a certain old-world mood. We talked about decorating the lodge in the style of a bygone era. Some of these pieces would fit perfectly."

He cupped his chin between thumb and forefinger. "Especially if we decorate the other converted stables in the Pacific style of the same period, so both cultures are represented." He patted her shoulder enthusiastically. "I'm sure Josquin can provide us with some artifacts from the period, on permanent loan from the royal collection."

His casual touch and ready use of the "us" almost stopped her in her tracks. She had become so carried away envisioning the lovely old pieces in their scheme, she had forgotten she wouldn't be here to see the result.

"I'm sure everything will work out perfectly," she said, unable to keep her tone from cooling with regret.

"Not quite perfectly," he commented. "You still haven't agreed to manage the lodge. We make a good team, Cris. We should continue as we are."

She took refuge in humor. "And give you time to get tired of me? No way."

"I seriously doubt that would happen."

So did she. That's why she had to leave. From the moment Eduard pulled her into his arms, thinking she was an intruder, she had felt the renewed tug of reaction.

Telling herself it was only the residue of her teenage crush didn't explain the instant, powerful desire that swept through her when she was around him. Like wildfire consuming a tinder-dry forest, the sensation threatened every bit of resistance she possessed.

If she hadn't had her baby to think of...she would do what? Throw herself at Eduard as stupidly as she had done once before? Surely she had learned something from that experience? Strange how her mind refused to accept it where Eduard was concerned.

He covered the rocking chair again. "We've been up here long enough. Ready for something to eat?"

Could the gnawing sensation inside her be hunger? These days her appetite was so unpredictable that she wouldn't be surprised. She nodded. "Your turn to cook dinner, as I recall."

"Then I vote for barbecue. Man-sized steaks, charcoal outside and still mooing inside, with baked potatoes and sour cream."

Her stomach recoiled at the thought of such a combination. "I'll make a salad," she volunteered. That way she could be sure of having something she could tolerate.

He caught the reluctance in her tone. "I thought you liked thick, juicy steak?"

"That was last week." Last week she had also wanted the meat smothered in cranberry sauce. She wasn't sure he believed her story that it was how they ate steak in Australia, but he had gone along with it. This week, she could barely stand the smell of meat cooking.

He regarded her keenly. "If you're still unwell, you should have said something before we came up here."

"I'm fine, really," she insisted. As long as he didn't wave a slab of steak under her nose.

The barbecue area was located beneath a pergola supporting a magnificent creeper that hadn't been pruned in two years. As a result, it was lush enough to keep the tropical rain off the cobbled paving, and at night, the air was thick with its scent, as heady as any perfume.

She had watched Eduard clean the barbecue grill a couple of days after he arrived. With his energy directed at the task, she had been able to look her fill. Hard to believe he was an heir to the throne of Valmont, cousin to the ruler of Carramer. He looked so approachable that her throat dried in an involuntary response.

He had looked up and caught her watching him. "Never seen a man clean a barbecue before?" he'd asked good-humoredly.

"Not a marquis, anyway," she'd retorted, her tone telling him she was impressed by the efficient way he worked. "Where did you learn to do chores like that?"

He had grinned. "The navy is no respecter of titles.

As a new recruit, I was expected to do my share of the grunt work like everyone else.''

He hadn't sounded as though he minded. "Did you ever wish you weren't royal?" she had asked.

He'd paused. "I don't care for the pomp and ceremony, but considering the good my position allows me to do, I can't really object.''

She heard him whistling now as he got the barbecue ready. The absence of guards and staff would have told her, if he hadn't, that he preferred to fend for himself. It was a quality she admired in him. One of a long list.

The phone's beeping interrupted her reverie. Trust someone to call when she was up to her elbows washing greens for the salad, she thought. Eduard's continued whistling told her he hadn't heard it.

Drying her hands on a towel, she draped it over her shoulder and picked up the receiver. "Tiga Falls Lodge.''

"Carissa, it's good to hear your voice.''

She tightened her hold on the phone. "How did you get this number, Mark?''

Her coldness was wasted on him. "Your brother gave it to me, after I told him I made a mistake letting you go.''

"You didn't let me go. I walked out.''

"Your news caught me by surprise, that's all. In the heat of the moment, we all say things we don't mean. I've had time to think things over, and I kind of like the idea of fatherhood.''

More likely he liked the idea of her having royal connections, she thought. Mark had always had an eye for the main chance. She had told Jeff she was working with Eduard, without telling him how she had been duped out of her nest egg. She felt foolish enough as it was, without her brother knowing the whole sorry story. She hoped Jeff hadn't told Mark where she was. It was bad enough that he had her number.

"Isn't your change of heart a bit sudden?" she asked him.

"Better late than never. I want to come to Carramer and see if we can make a fresh start."

"There's no point. After the vile suggestion you made about my baby, I don't want to see you again."

"Our baby," he reminded her coolly. "You can't deny me a say in my child's future."

"Last time we spoke, you didn't even want a child."

"When did I say that?"

"When you offered me money to solve the problem, as you so charmingly expressed it."

He gave a low laugh. "And you thought I meant…heck, Carissa, I only meant you'd need money for doctors and the like."

She knew exactly what kind of doctor he'd meant. "Don't lie, and don't bother getting on a plane on my account. You're wasting your time." But she was talking to the hum of a dead line.

Chapter Five

Mark's call continued to trouble Carissa as she carried a tray out to the terrace where Eduard was supervising the barbecue. Deep in thought, she began to set the table. She couldn't stop Mark from following her, but she hated the thought of another confrontation. No way had she misunderstood him when he'd offered her money, and she would never forgive him for that. What was she to make of his sudden reversal?

Nothing, she decided, hoping she'd sounded cool enough on the phone to deter him from coming. Tiga Falls was a long way from anywhere. Even if he found out where she was, he might decide it wasn't worth the trip.

Eduard expertly turned a piece of steak, making it sizzle. Looking around him, he said, "I missed all this while I was away in the navy."

Carissa, too, had been captivated by the beauty and serenity at first sight. "I can understand why."

"My brother never could. If he wasn't climbing the hills, he wanted to be swimming or hiking."

"You're not exactly sedentary yourself," she pointed out.

"True, but there are times to be on the move and times to be still. When I come here, I enjoy the stillness. At night you can practically hear it."

She knew what he meant. Coming from Sydney, which had the perpetual background hum common to most thriving cities, she had marveled at the depth of the silence at the lodge. It reminded her of the still, clear nights she'd enjoyed in Switzerland. Few places in the world made her feel so tranquil. She wasn't looking forward to leaving.

As she had expected, the glistening meat Eduard brought to the table made her shudder, but she heaped her plate with salad. She might have known she wouldn't get away without some comment.

"If you don't eat something more substantial than that, I'm going to take you to the doctor in Tricot myself," Eduard admonished.

"I'm too tired to eat," she said truthfully, but made a valiant effort.

"Which doesn't explain why you look washed-out first thing in the morning. Did you think I hadn't noticed?"

She put her fork down. "Why do men always feel that their gender gives them the right to tell women what's best for them?"

Before he could respond, she walked away from the pool of light into the moonlit garden. Shadows flickered at her feet as tree branches swayed in the soft breeze. When she brushed past the bushes, the scent of night-blooming jasmine perfumed the air.

Her problem wasn't Eduard, it was Mark, she knew. If not for his threat to follow her to Carramer, she would have been blissfully content. She had never dreamed that he would decide to take an interest in the baby now.

A new thought made her stumble. What would she do if he tried to gain custody of her child? As owner of the lodge, with a secure home and future, she could have fought him with a fair chance of winning. Now, she had no home or income, and falling prey to a con man hardly made her appear a vision of competence.

On the other hand, Mark managed to look every inch the successful businessman, no matter how his fortunes were running. And she knew first-hand how charming he could be. She splayed her hands over her stomach, fancying she could feel a slight swelling there, although she knew it was too soon. "Nobody is going to take you away from me," she vowed softly. "We'll manage, somehow."

"What will you manage?" came a voice close behind her.

She started, not having heard Eduard come after her. She turned. Moonlight glinted off his hair, threading the rich chestnut strands with gold highlights. His eyes were dark with concern and for a moment she was tempted to unburden herself to him. But there was nothing he could do. This was her problem and it was up to her to solve it.

"I was thinking aloud," she said.

"You have a home here for as long as you need one, if that's what's on your mind."

She plucked a leaf from a fragrant bush and crushed it between her fingers, the lavender-like scent soothing her. The bush was a Carramer native, and she wondered distractedly if the leaves had herbal qualities. Maybe they could make sachets of the leaves to place in drawers and on pillows, adding to the old-world atmosphere.

She almost laughed at herself. She should be planning how she could use what money she had left to find a new home for herself and her baby. Instead, she was still preoccupied with the lodge.

Eduard saw her smile. "The idea of staying pleases you. Good."

Letting the fragrant leaf fall to the ground, she said, "It's more tempting than you can possibly imagine."

"But you won't take me up on it."

"I can't. This place belongs to you."

"No reason we can't share. When it was Prince Henry's, most of the family was in residence at different times. I'm not used to having it all to myself."

"You'll have plenty of company when the paying guests start arriving. I'm sure they'll be thrilled that their host is a real live marquis."

He winced. "I don't intend to play that much of a hands-on role. You'd make a much better host."

She glanced away, shaking her head. "All my life I've wanted a real home, where I never have to move again." When she had started planning to move to Carramer, she had dreamed of putting down roots. Mark had seemed to share her enthusiasm—that was, until he'd learned about the baby.

Eduard came closer, traces of his aftershave lotion adding a note of pine to the night scents. "You could consider this your home."

Her senses swam, making it difficult to focus her thoughts. "It's not the same. Can you imagine what it's like always to live in an embassy house, knowing that after a year or two you have to move on?''

''Only slightly, through my experiences in the navy. My roots go back so far that I feel as if Carramer is part of me.''

''That's the way I want to feel. For me and…'' She stopped herself before she said ''me and my baby.''

His gaze grew hooded as he filled in the gap himself. ''The man you mentioned sharing the lodge with?''

She didn't know yet whether her baby was a boy or a girl, so she could answer truthfully. ''I haven't decided.''

''What's this man's name?''

She debated whether to make something up, then decided to stick to the facts. ''I was seeing a man called Mark Lucas. He works with my brother in the money market.''

Eduard pushed aside an overhanging branch screening her expression from him. ''You said 'was.' Sounds like past tense to me.''

Why did he care? ''If you must know, he called me this evening,'' she said with a toss of her head.

''I thought I heard the phone. What's your Mark Lucas like?''

She didn't want to talk about Mark, and especially not to Eduard. Forcing a smile, she said, ''What is this, the third degree? You sound like my big brother.''

''Is that such a bad thing?''

Better than sounding like a lover, she told herself, torn between relief that Eduard evidently saw his interest in her as brotherly, and resentment because she didn't want him in that role.

She was almost afraid to ask herself what she did want from him.

"You're right," he said, breaking the spell. "It's none of my business." He hooked his thumbs into his belt and she had the oddest feeling he was struggling to keep his hands away from her. She shivered. What had happened to brotherly? The air between them felt charged with a force like electricity.

When he took her hand, she half expected to see flames leap between them. But nothing happened, although warmth spread through her from his fingers. "You've had a rough deal, Cris. If there was a way for me to give you the lodge, I would. But I can't as long as I hold it in trust for my...for future generations."

She caught the hesitation, sure he had been about to say "for my children." Didn't he want to have children? Somehow she had always pictured Eduard surrounded by sons who looked just like him, and perhaps a little girl who looked like...no, she forced the thought away. Eduard's plans didn't concern her. She had enough problems worrying about her own.

"We've already agreed that the lodge belongs in the royal family," she said tautly, barely stopping herself from swaying toward him. What was she doing, holding hands with him in a rain-forest clearing painted by moonlight? The setting was dangerously romantic.

He felt her try to pull away, but kept his fingers in hers. She reminded him of a sun deer, easily put to flight. He couldn't accept that their discussion about the lodge had made her this edgy. The call from Mark Lucas had to be part of it. Eduard wished he knew more about the relationship. Was she still involved with Lucas? The man had called her, so he must want the involvement, perhaps more than Cris did. That she was here alone seemed to prove it. If Eduard had been in

Lucas's shoes, he would never have let her travel half-way across the Pacific without him.

He was hardly in a position to criticize, he reminded himself. He had almost said he was keeping the lodge in trust for his children. But no offspring of his would explore these woods as he had done as a boy. They would never fill the lodge with their laughter and their constant activity.

For him, there would be no offspring.

He didn't regret his part in the sea rescue that had robbed him of the chance at fatherhood. Given the same circumstances, he would do exactly what he had done the first time. One of the men he had plucked from the chemical soup was a father of five children all under eight, and Eduard had seen the family's faces when they were reunited. No regrets.

Until then, he had always imagined himself fathering children one day. Now that dream was uncertain and he didn't know what he had to offer a woman in its place. Until he did, marriage was not for him.

Maybe it was for the best if Lucas was still on the scene. It meant Eduard could help and support Carissa without worrying about getting romantically involved.

Again the sun deer image came to him. He would have to be gentle with her if he hoped to get close enough to help her. She had accused him of acting like her big brother. Was that the answer? Should he act more like a brother toward her and hope she opened up to him?

A savage feeling of denial tore through him. In spite of his good intentions, he didn't want her thinking of him in that way. Against all reason, he wanted a repeat of the experience outside the Mayat cave, when he had taken her in his arms and kissed her fiercely. He wanted to do it again, right here in the moonlight. Beneath their feet, a carpet of fallen leaves would make a soft bed where they could enjoy the night sounds and scents, and one another. When he finished showing her what they could be together, she would have no thought for any other man but Eduard himself.

So much for brotherly.

"Let's walk," he said, his tone hoarse with needs he was having trouble keeping to himself.

She hesitated. "Don't we need a torch?"

"The moonlight will light our way. I grew up roaming these paths by day and night."

"I'll bet your nanny didn't know about the night part."

"You're right." He turned her around so she could look back at the lodge. How slender she felt, how delicate. He marshaled his thoughts with an effort. "See that third window from the left?"

Light from the window spilled over the scene. "The one with the old ironwood growing alongside it?"

"After I was supposed to be asleep, I would climb out that window and down the tree."

She lifted an eyebrow. "What happened to enjoying the stillness?"

His look asked her to give him a break. "What do ten-year-olds know about keeping still?"

Not much if they were all like Eduard, she thought. He might credit Mathiaz with being more active, but if memory served, Eduard had seldom settled for long when he was younger. From the passion with which he attacked his plans for the lodge, she had already seen how little he had changed in that respect. When her own child was older, would he be as full of vitality? Or she? Carissa didn't really have a preference.

Knowing how much she wanted this child, she was alarmed at her growing tendency to connect the child with Eduard. Was she unconsciously searching for a father figure for her baby? Or was her agenda more personal?

Either way, the situation wouldn't be helped by walking with him in the moonlight. "I'll take a rain check."

He leaned closer. "Would you like me to come back inside and keep you company?"

That was the last thing she needed. "Thanks, but I'll be fine."

"Then I'll stretch my legs, and help you with the cleaning up when I get back."

By the time he returned, she had taken care of the dishes. She was folding the tablecloth when he walked in. He surveyed the tidy kitchen. "Couldn't wait, could you?"

She hadn't wanted to wait, afraid that sharing the chore with him might inflame the desire she already felt building whenever he was with her. Doing dishes together might not be the most romantic task, but any sort of closeness with Eduard was starting to get to her.

Like now for instance.

Outside, night had made the lodge into an island. The stars shone impossibly bright in a black velvet sky and night birds called from the rain forest. She found the sounds more comforting than alarming, as if they were letting her know she had friends all around her.

Inside, there was only her and Eduard.

He looked annoyed. "No wonder you're overtired. I didn't ask you to stay because I needed a housemaid."

"I'm used to cleaning up after myself. I didn't grow up with servants at my beck and call."

"Unlike me," he interpreted, his tone a low growl.

She was too on edge after Mark's call to heed the warning. "If the shoe fits…"

He stalked toward her, his expression angry. Then he stopped cold. "This isn't like you, Cris. You've been a nervous wreck since you got that phone call. Lucas isn't harassing you in some way, is he?"

She wished she could say yes. It was true in a way. But it would mean explaining why Mark wanted to see her. She wasn't ready for that yet. Or to face Eduard's disappointment in her.

That he might not be disappointed, but would insist on helping her, was even more disturbing. The way she felt around him, she wasn't prepared to take the risk. She shifted from foot to foot, not meeting his gaze. "We parted on bad terms. I didn't expect to hear from him again." All true as far as it went.

"And now?"

"I don't know." Also true.

In a swift move, Eduard was beside her, and she was in his arms, melting against him as she had wanted to do all evening. Her head fitted perfectly in the hollow between his neck and shoulder, and she felt the powerful beat of his heart resonating through her.

In storage with her things, she had a soft toy that emitted a beat like a human heart, designed to reassure a baby. Now she knew why it was so effective. The steady thrum of Eduard's heartbeat was like a promise that everything would work out.

She sighed. Whether she believed that or not, she needed this moment to regroup. In just a few seconds, she would free herself from his embrace and go to bed. Alone.

The seconds stretched into minutes. The feel of his

hand stroking her hair was so good that she wanted to purr. Breathing shallowly, he lowered his lips to her hairline in the merest brush of a kiss.

Flames leaped inside her in an instant, powerful response. Closing her eyes, she let her head drop back. Shuddering, he cupped her face in both hands and kissed her parted lips. With a groan that sounded like surrender, he gathered her into his arms.

She felt her own kind of surrender, and told herself it was only to the comfort he was offering. Her life was already complicated enough without this.

He buried his face in her hair, murmuring softly in the Carramer language. She knew enough to recognize the endearments and feel resistance kick in. He was going way past comfort into dangerous territory she was far from ready to explore. She tensed.

He felt her reaction and lifted his head, his eyes bright. "I know, we shouldn't."

Knowing he was right, and convincing her errant body were two different things. When he released her she forced herself to step away, to pick up a cloth and polish the crystal glassware.

He watched the grace with which she performed the simple chore. His heartbeat was racing, and the heat tearing through him told him how close he had come to violating his intention to treat her as a sister. His brisk walk through the rain forest had been meant to cool his ardor. Instead, the fragrant night scents and the seductive moonlight had inflamed him until he could hardly wait to return and take her in his arms.

"Maybe it's better if you do leave," he said, half to himself.

Shock radiated through her in waves. She hadn't expected that. He'd tried so hard to talk her into staying and working for him, that she had begun to wonder if that was her answer after all. Now hearing him say he wanted her to go robbed her of breath for a moment. She recovered enough to say, "If it's what you want."

He gave her an enigmatic look. "It's the opposite of what I want, as you must know. Being alone here isn't a good idea."

She could hardly argue, given how close she had just come to begging him to make love to her. "No, it isn't."

"There is another option. I could be the one to leave."

She twisted the dish towel into a rope. "I wouldn't feel comfortable, knowing I've driven you away from your own property."

He gave a rueful half smile. "Better that than what we risk happening if I stay."

She had her own reasons for discouraging his attention, although the little success she'd had so far was almost laughable. But why was Eduard determined not to get involved with her? Was there another woman in his life?

She realized she knew very little about him beyond his public image. She had followed his exploits in the navy, been aware of the publicity that dogged any royal bachelor, but he had guarded his privacy jealously. The thought that he might be in love with someone hit her like a dash of cold water.

She busied herself putting the glasses away. "I'm sorry, I should have thought..."

He closed the cupboard door firmly, giving her no choice but to face him. "What should you have thought?"

Strange how hard it was to say. "That you might

want to bring a woman here, and my presence is stopping you.''

Amusement danced across his even features. ''Jealous, Cris?''

Annoyed at being the object of his amusement, she felt heat steal into her face. ''Of course not. You're entitled to bring whomever you wish to the lodge.'' Even to herself, the denial sounded unconvincing.

He rested his back against the cupboard and folded his arms. ''What if I told you she's already here?''

Her jealousy evaporated, replaced by confusion. ''Then why did you say I should leave?''

''For both our sakes. You're obviously not over Lucas yet, and even if you decide you are, I'm not the man for you. The longer you remain here with me, the greater the risk I'll forget it, as we so nearly demonstrated.''

How well she knew that danger. Her heartbeat was still racing, and her lips tingled from the effects of his kiss. He had to mean that he couldn't get involved with her because of his royal status, and her spirits plunged at the thought. It was the one argument she couldn't refute.

She felt cool suddenly, although the night was warm. Clearing her throat, she said, ''You're right, I should go.''

''But not yet.''

''You just said…''

''We're both grown-ups, Cris.''

Not like the first time, she thought. The first time she'd kissed him, she had been stranded in the limbo between childhood and womanhood, unable to deal with her feelings for him. A teenager himself, he hadn't known how to respond. Now he was crediting them both with the maturity to handle temptation without giving in to it. She wished she shared his confidence.

"True," she agreed stiffly.

"Then we can work together, share the lodge, and still keep our emotional distance?"

Hurt because it was obviously what he preferred, she affected a shrug. "If it's what you want."

He crossed the kitchen and closed the door, locking it, then turned to her. "It's what we both need. You look tired. Let's go to bed."

For a moment her body quivered in response, but only for a moment. He was right. She was grown up now, no longer at the mercy of her impulses, however powerful. Fantasizing about Eduard, when his royal status made any sort of future impossible, was useless.

However, there was one impulse she could act on. Tomorrow she would start looking for a real job and a place of her own. She had to think of her baby. Waiting around to see what Mark might do would play right into his hands. If she could show that she was able to support herself and her child, Mark would find it much more difficult to interfere in their lives.

And Eduard would never have to know the reason why she had to leave.

She made her feet carry her out of the kitchen. Eduard followed her down the hallway, turning off lights as they went. At her bedroom door he touched her cheek and bade her goodnight, before going into his own room.

With one hand resting on the doorknob, she lifted the other and touched the path his fingers had traced over her face. Her insides churned as if she had just stepped off a roller-coaster ride. Had she actually stepped off it, or was this only the breath-stealing pause at the top of a steep grade, before the ride hurtled on again?

She went into her room, closing the door on the thought.

Chapter Six

She hadn't counted on heavy rain setting in for the next two days, preventing her from stepping outside the lodge, far less start hunting for a new home and job. Eduard didn't share her restlessness. He locked himself away in his study with his portable computer, catching up on work for the Merrisand Trust, he told her, when he emerged at mealtimes.

The respite gave her a chance to update her resumé, and make a few calls to hotels in Valmont Province. They weren't encouraging about job openings, but suggested she leave her details with them in case something came up in the future.

Fortunately Mark hadn't called again. She began to think he wasn't going to, although she recognized an element of wishful thinking in this. Her life was complicated enough without him adding to her worries.

To her relief, the third morning dawned bright and clear, the sky an impossibly blue canopy overhead. Exactly the sort of day Carissa had dreamed about when she had decided to make Carramer her home. Before her father had been posted here, they'd lived in London for two years, under pewter skies that made Carissa yearn for the sunshine and vivid colors of the southern hemisphere.

If she hadn't woken up feeling so wretched, she would have been up watching the sunrise and listening to the chorus of birds welcoming the dawn.

She hadn't felt this ill before, and she knew her makeup didn't compensate for her pallor when she finally staggered into the kitchen to make breakfast.

Every other morning, by the time she had gotten up, Eduard had eaten and retreated to his study to work. She sighed inwardly as she found him lingering over a cup of coffee, a plate of toast at his elbow. Why did he have to pick today to alter his routine?

He was dressed all in dark blue, she noticed. Body-hugging navy sweater and narrow-legged jeans the color of midnight, over suede loafers. Fabric patches on the shoulders of his sweater suggested navy issue.

He looked like navy issue, too, his back ramrod-straight even when he was relaxing over breakfast. She could picture him on a ship somewhere, leaping into his helicopter from a heaving deck, then lifting off into the blue yonder.

She found it easier to imagine him like that than on some royal engagement. He did both, she knew, moving between his two worlds with ease. Her eyes traced the broad sweep of his shoulder, the strong column of his neck. Sunshine spilling into the room edged his dark hair with an aura of gold. She turned away abruptly, her hands trembling.

He saw her reach for the toaster. "Have some of this. I made plenty."

The thick slabs of bread he had generously buttered made her shudder. "Do you know what that stuff does to your cholesterol level?"

He raised a challenging eyebrow. "According to the royal physician and the navy doctors, my cholesterol level is exemplary." To emphasize the point, he bit into a slice and licked butter off his fingers.

The sight almost had her racing for the bathroom again until she got her heaving stomach under control. Turning away, she began to make fresh toast. Fresh, *dry* toast.

"What about yours?" he asked unexpectedly.

The toast shot out of the toaster and she caught it, the heat making her fumble it, fortunately onto her plate. She carried it to the table and sat down opposite him, avoiding the unnerving directness of his gaze. "What about my what?"

"Your cholesterol level, among other things."

She reached for the orange juice on the table. He forestalled her by pouring her a cup of coffee. In passing, his hand brushed hers and her stomach churned again, but with a different sensation this time. Pleasure, she recognized. The desire to have him touch her again, more intimately. And not to stop at touching.

Her pulse fluttered wildly. No amount of reminding herself that she was a grown-up and supposedly able to handle the closeness had the least effect on the tumult inside her.

She tucked her hands into her lap. "I'm as healthy as a horse."

"A very fragile horse. When was the last time you took a vacation?"

Knowing how pale she looked, it was a fair question. She had started her last job within days of returning to

Australia, throwing herself into a demanding six-days-a-week schedule without a second thought.

Until she came to Carramer, most of her free time had been taken up with Mark, who liked to party hard. Not for him walks on the beach or rain-forest picnics. He fretted if he didn't have a crowd around him. When they were together, she had joked about needing to go to work to catch her breath.

Her father's death had spurred her to work harder to deal with the intensity of her sorrow. A vacation had been a long way down her list.

"It's been a while," she admitted. "When you're doing work you enjoy, it doesn't seem to matter."

Eduard picked up his plate and cup and carried them to the dishwasher. "That isn't the point. Everybody has a limit, and from the look of you, you're close to reaching yours."

She nibbled on the toast. "I'm fine, really." For a mother-to-be.

He came back and placed both hands flat on the table beside her. "News for you, Cris. You're on vacation as of now."

"I planned to do some more work in the kitchen garden." She had intended to finish clearing the beds ready for replanting.

"I'll take care of the garden. Consider this a royal command."

She gave him an irritated look. "The Marquis of Merrisand has spoken?"

He shrugged. "The title has to be good for something."

"It's good for doing important work for charity."

"Well, now it has an extra purpose."

"Keeping me in line," she said. "What happens if I refuse to obey your royal command?"

He regarded her gravely. "I'm sure I can think of a suitable penalty."

She set her coffee cup down and met his look with a challenging one of her own. "Will I be banished from the kingdom? Cast into the sea? What?"

He crossed his arms, his brows drawn together although his eyes under them sparked with humor. "There's a little thing called a personal bond, used in ancient times by Carramer royalty to keep recalcitrants in line."

Her nerves jangled at the intimacy such a tie represented. She swallowed hard, resisting the image. "Didn't I hear that when they first met, Prince Lorne imposed such a bond on Princess Alison to keep her from leaving Carramer, so he would have a chance to propose to her?"

Eduard nodded. "If it's good enough for the monarch…"

She subsided in her seat, wondering whether he was referring to the bond or the proposal. She decided he had to mean the bond. "Then I'd better behave myself, hadn't I?"

"My point precisely." He rejoined her at the table, pushing the neglected plate of toast closer to her. "The personal bond has only one drawback."

She picked up a piece of toast and bit into it, finding she could think of several drawbacks. Which one troubled Eduard? "I have the feeling you're about to enlighten me."

"The bonded person is under the protection of the one imposing the bond. Our law prohibits any kind of intimacy between them."

She almost choked on the toast. Here she had been worried about the closeness implied by the bond, when the very opposite was true. "Didn't that makes things rather awkward for Prince Lorne with Princess Alison?"

The corners of Eduard's mouth twitched. "Probably why my dear cousin revoked the bond so quickly."

From what she had seen and heard of Prince Lorne, he was powerfully attractive to women, an appeal Carissa had no trouble understanding, given the way Eduard made her feel. Must be genetic, she decided, since Lorne and Eduard were first cousins.

Hearsay had it that from the moment Carissa's countrywoman, Alison Carter, had arrived in Carramer, the monarch had had eyes only for her. Their marriage was one of the happiest in the kingdom and had given Carramer two heirs to the throne. Carissa could imagine the stress of feeling so attracted to someone, only to be legally bound to keep your distance.

If the bond were between her and Eduard…

Stop this, she instructed herself angrily. He had only mentioned the penalty to persuade her to relax. She wasn't likely to provoke him into imposing any sanctions against her of that kind, so the problem wouldn't arise. They had already agreed to be mature about the attraction simmering between them, so they needed no legal strictures to keep them apart.

She rested her chin on one hand. "Carramer has some interesting laws." Like the one prohibiting divorce, she knew.

He nodded. "As an island kingdom, we've tended to make up our own rules as we've gone along."

"You've never been tempted to change the rules?"

"For myself?"

'For anyone. I heard that Prince Lorne's first marriage was desperately unhappy. Why didn't he simply change the law so he could get a divorce?''

''He preferred to set a good example by trying to work things out.''

If Lorne's first wife hadn't died in a car accident, they would still be married and unhappy, she concluded. Or *would* they have worked things out and had a stronger marriage as a result? ''Do you agree with your cousin?'' she asked.

Eduard looked thoughtful. ''As a member of the ruling family, I uphold our laws. They've served us well for a thousand years.''

She wasn't going to get any more out of him, she saw, understanding why he was determined to approach any relationship with caution. Would people in other countries rush into marriage if they knew it was for life, as it was in Carramer?

Without thinking, she took a sip of coffee, winced at its strength, and pushed the cup away. ''How can you drink this stuff? And how long is this royal-command vacation supposed to last?'' Not long enough to hinder her plan to find a new job and home for herself, she hoped. Otherwise she might have to defy him and hope he didn't seriously mean to put her under bond to him.

He took her plate and cup to the sink and emptied out the coffee. ''A few days ought to be enough to put some color back into your face.''

She regarded him with as much dismay as if he had suggested a sojourn in jail. ''A few days? What am I supposed to do for that length of time?''

''Relax, put your feet up. Read a book. Prince Henry left a well-stocked library, if you like the classics.''

"As it happens, I do." She'd already explored the library during her first days here. "*After* I put in a good day's work."

"You could explore some of the gentler walks around the lodge."

She stood up and stretched. "I'd really rather keep working in the garden."

She turned toward the door, but he grabbed her hand and swung her around. "It's not too late for me to impose that bond, you know."

A longing for him gripped her as tightly as his hold on her hand, threatening to drag her beneath the surface of its treacherous currents. She could swear she felt flames flash from his fingertips, along the length of her arm, singeing a path to her heart.

Her emotions spun, making her wonder for a heartbeat whether she was as recovered from her bout of morning sickness as she'd thought. These were pleasurable sensations, alarming in their intensity and suddenness, but undeniably pleasurable.

Struggling against the sensations, she brought her free hand to his chest, needing to put some distance between them. He looked down at the hand holding him at bay, his expression unreadable.

Carissa closed her eyes. "Maybe the bond isn't such a bad idea after all."

His breath rasped in her ears. "Explain."

"If it forces us to keep our distance."

"Do you think that could ever be sufficient?"

Hearing the tension in his voice, she forced her eyes open and was shaken by the depth of desire she glimpsed, but only for a second until his gaze became hooded again.

She must have imagined the desire. Or at least the

emotion powering it. He might want her physically, but he was no better than Mark in not wanting her in his life. He had made that clear enough when he reminded her of the difference in their status, and nothing had changed.

So where did that leave her?

Standing on her own two feet, that's where. However bleak her future looked, she refused to let herself think of Eduard as a solution. The closer she allowed him to come, the more angry he was likely to be when he found out her secret.

She tugged on the hand imprisoning hers, but he didn't release her. "I want to know what's bothering you, Cris."

Her breathing tightened. Couldn't he see how hard he was making this for her? She tried to make her tone light. "What makes you think anything's bothering me?"

He wasn't fooled. "No one looks as pale and fragile as you do, unless something's the matter." An expression of shock crossed his face as he reached his own conclusion. "Are you ill? Is that why you ran away to Carramer?"

Good grief, she'd managed to give him the impression that she had a terminal illness and had come here to spend her last days. If he hadn't looked so worried, she would have laughed. Although the outcome of her condition would be with her for the rest of her life, it wasn't usually terminal.

She managed to get herself under control. "I give you my word that I'm not ill."

He gave an audible sigh of relief, but she saw his jaw harden. "I'm not letting you off the hook that eas-

PLAY

LUCKY HEARTS

GAME

AND YOU GET

- ◆ **FREE BOOKS!**
- ◆ **A FREE GIFT!**
- ◆ **YOURS TO KEEP!**

TURN THE PAGE AND DEAL YOURSELF IN...

Play **LUCKY HEARTS** for this..

exciting FREE gift!
This surprise mystery gift could be yours free

when you play **LUCKY HEARTS!**
...then continue your lucky streak with a sweetheart of a deal!

1. Play Lucky Hearts as instructed on the opposite page.

2. Send back this card and you'll receive 2 brand-new Silhouette Romance® books. These books have a cover price of $3.99 each in the U.S., and $4.50 each in Canada, but they are yours to keep absolutely free.

3. There's no catch! You're under no obligation to buy anything. We charge nothing—ZERO—for your first shipment. And you don't have to make any minimum number of purchases—not even one!

4. The fact is thousands of readers enjoy receiving their books by mail from the Silhouette Reader Service™. They enjoy the convenience of home delivery...they like getting the best new novels at discount prices, BEFORE they're available in stores...and they love their *Heart to Heart* subscriber newsletter featuring author news, horoscopes, recipes, book reviews and much more!

5. We hope that after receiving your free books you'll want to remain a subscriber. But the choice is yours—to continue or cancel, any time at all! So why not take us up on our invitation, with no risk of any kind. You'll be glad you did!

Visit us online at
www.eHarlequin.com

- ♦ **Exciting Silhouette® romance books— FREE!**
- ♦ **Plus an exciting mystery gift—FREE!**
- ♦ **No cost! No obligation to buy!**

YES!

I have scratched off the silver card. Please send me the 2 FREE books and gift for which I qualify. I understand I am under no obligation to purchase any books, as explained on the back and on the opposite page.

With a coin, scratch off the silver card and check below to see what we have for you.

LUCKY HEARTS GAME

315 SDL DRN6   **215 SDL DRPP**

FIRST NAME

| LAST NAME |

| ADDRESS |

| APT.# | CITY |

| STATE/PROV. | ZIP/POSTAL CODE |

Twenty-one gets you 2 free books, and a free mystery gift!

Twenty gets you 2 free books!

Nineteen gets you 1 free book!

Try Again!

Offer limited to one per household and not valid to current Silhouette Romance® subscribers. All orders subject to approval.

(S-R-12/02)

The Silhouette Reader Service™—Here's how it works:

Accepting your 2 free books and gift places you under no obligation to buy anything. You may keep the books and gift and return the shipping statement marked "cancel." If you do not cancel, about a month later we'll send you 6 additional books and bill you just $3.34 each in the U.S., or $3.80 each in Canada, plus 25¢ shipping & handling per book and applicable taxes if any.* That's the complete price and — compared to cover prices of $3.99 each in the U.S. and $4.50 each in Canada — it's quite a bargain! You may cancel at any time, but if you choose to continue, every month we'll send you 6 more books, which you may either purchase at the discount price or return to us and cancel your subscription.

*Terms and prices subject to change without notice. Sales tax applicable in N.Y. Canadian residents will be charged applicable provincial taxes and GST.

If offer card is missing write to: Silhouette Reader Service, 3010 Walden Ave., P.O. Box 1867, Buffalo, NY 14240-1867

BUSINESS REPLY MAIL
FIRST-CLASS MAIL   PERMIT NO. 717-003   BUFFALO, NY

POSTAGE WILL BE PAID BY ADDRESSEE

SILHOUETTE READER SERVICE
3010 WALDEN AVE
PO BOX 1867
BUFFALO NY 14240-9952

NO POSTAGE
NECESSARY
IF MAILED
IN THE
UNITED STATES

ily. Come outside, we're going to talk, and you're going to tell me what's going on.''

He made it sound like an invitation, but he kept hold of her hand as he led her outside into the sunlight. Her heart triple-timed. She hated the thought of facing his censure, but couldn't see any way out of telling him what he wanted to know.

He steered her to a wrought-iron bench under the ironwood tree he'd climbed as a boy. His and his brother's initials were incised into the trunk, she noticed. They were so weathered that she could barely make them out.

Eduard saw her looking at them and ran his fingers over the faint impression. ''When our father found this, he was furious. He told us when we could create something as enduring as this tree, we'd be entitled to put our mark on it, and not before.''

''Your father is a wise man,'' she observed, remembering how Prince Claude had treated her and Jeffrey almost as members of his family.

Eduard shook his head. ''Not always. But that particular piece of advice stayed with me ever since, because he was right.''

She took the seat he indicated. ''We can't all create monuments.''

He sat down beside her. ''I believe he was referring to achievements more than buildings or statues.''

The bench was barely wide enough for two adults, and his muscular thigh pressed against hers. He seemed unaware of the contact, or of the havoc it loosed inside her. Taking a deep breath, she steadied her voice. ''Your father could also have meant children. They endure long after we conceive them.'' Possibly into history, if the child was remarkable enough, she thought.

"I wouldn't know about that."

She recoiled from his cold tone. His mood had changed the last time she mentioned children, she recalled. In Eduard's position, she knew he must be expected to produce heirs to inherit his land and titles. Perhaps his parents had been pressuring him about his single status, and her comments had touched a nerve.

She touched his hand lightly. "I'm sorry if I spoke out of turn."

"You didn't." His expression cleared but his tone remained distant. "This isn't about me. I want to know what's bothering you."

She wished they hadn't gone off at a tangent. His reaction to the mention of children made her even more reluctant to admit the truth. Coward, she rebuked herself. The problem wasn't with Eduard but with her. She didn't want him to know the extent of her foolishness. Her brother had left her in no doubt about what he thought, especially when she explained that she wasn't going to marry the father of her baby.

"How many men do you think will want you once you tell them you have a child?" Jeff had demanded. "You'd do better to work things out with Mark while you still can."

Jeff hadn't wanted to hear about Mark's role in the breakup. She suspected that Jeff didn't know Mark as well as he thought he did, or he wouldn't be so keen to see her married to his friend.

Her brother had looked at her as if she had taken leave of her senses, using phrases like, "I never expected it of you, Cris." And the cruellest, "I'm glad Dad isn't around to hear about this." Wasn't there an equal chance that their father would have been happy at the prospect of his first grandchild? Evidently Jeff didn't think so.

She'd seen no point in reminding Jeff that marriage wasn't the only option open to women these days, but insisted she could take care of herself. He had played his trump card, pointing out that their father hadn't thought so, or he wouldn't have willed the house to Jeff with instructions to look after her.

Belatedly accepting that Jeff was every bit as chauvinistic as their father, she had known she was making the right choice in leaving. Only when he found he couldn't change her mind had Jeff offered her half the house's value in cash. She had thought he was being fair. Now she guessed he had been making peace with his conscience so he could wash his hands of her.

As no doubt Eduard would do once she told him the truth.

She got to her feet. "You're right. I do need a vacation. I'm sure after I take a few days off, I'll be fine."

"Sit down."

Whether acquired through royal tutelage, or during his service in the navy, his tone of command was snapped out in the full expectation that she would obey. But she wasn't one of his subjects, or serving under his command. She took a half step away.

His arm shot out, his fingers handcuffing her wrist before she could complete the move. "I asked you to sit down."

She gave a toss of her head, but her heart picked up speed again with the awareness of how effortlessly he restrained her. "You didn't ask, you ordered," she said, infuriated at having her self-control whittled to a thread by his touch.

He released her, but his expression remained set. "Force of habit. Please sit down."

She sat, wishing she could put more distance between them. He moved closer. "Something's troubling you, Cris. I can't help unless I know what the problem is."

Bleakly, she met his gaze. "I didn't ask for your help."

"You never did, even as a teenager. Do you remember your first attempt at sailboarding?"

"Only too painfully. I never got the hang of keeping the sailboard upright, and spent most of the time getting dunked."

"Yet when I came by in my boat and offered you a hand, you insisted you were fine."

With the self-consciousness of a girl on the verge of womanhood, she had hated him seeing her graceless performance. Bad enough that he had witnessed her clumsiness, without having him haul her out of the surf looking like a drowned cat. "I was fine," she insisted, "waterlogged, but fine."

"And I was too arrogant to get the message. You'd think with an older brother to witness my mistakes, I'd have understood how much it rankles to have a know-it-all around."

"Everything rankles when you're fifteen," she said. "And you were never a know-it-all."

"I'm acting like one now, prying into your affairs when you obviously resent the interference," he said softly.

"I don't..." she began.

He silenced her with a gesture. "Don't say any more. You're a grown woman now, not a teenager in need of guidance. If you do decide to share whatever's on your mind, I'm here."

She could hardly speak for the lump filling her throat. She was the interloper here. He was being kinder than she had any right to expect. "I never thought of you as arrogant or a know-it-all then, and I don't now."

He cleared his throat. "I suspect your opinion is about to change."

She tilted her head back, regarding him with suspicion. "Why should it?"

"Because I've made an appointment for you with Dr. Brunet in Tricot for later this morning."

She had seen the doctor soon after she arrived, but she wasn't yet due for another checkup. She narrowed her eyes. Dr. Brunet was the only doctor in Tricot, and very busy. "How could you get an appointment that quickly?"

He got up, looking as though he would like to pace, but held himself still. "Royal privilege."

She might have known. "I thought you said you're through giving me advice?"

"This isn't advice, it's common sense. You've promised me you're not ill, but what if there's something wrong that you don't know about? No one is as pale and listless as this for no reason."

"There is a good reason," she shouted at him, reaching the end of her tether. "I'm not ill, I'm pregnant."

Chapter Seven

She spun away, not stopping until she came to the herb bed she'd been putting to rights. Mindlessly she dropped to her knees and began to pull a few remaining weeds from around a clump of oregano that had somehow managed to thrive amid the overgrowth. As she intended to thrive, no matter how Eduard reacted to her admission.

She was aware of him following her, but kept at her task. Only when he gently lifted her to her feet was she unable to avoid facing him.

He was looking at her as if seeing her for the first time. Would she always think of him like this, standing with his estate at his back, a lord in the figurative as well as the literal sense? He had released her as soon as she regained her feet. Now he stood with his feet apart, hands braced on his hips, a man in a class by himself. "Did you just say what I thought you said?"

This wasn't how she had wanted to tell him, but she

couldn't take the declaration back. She had never wanted a man more, nor expected to touch him less.

As if she could escape the yearnings that now could never become reality, she stood up and paced to the edge of the kitchen garden, to where a wishing well was emerging as the undergrowth was cleared away. The well was a bit of whimsy someone had built there years before. Even Eduard had said he didn't remember seeing it, so perhaps it had been overgrown for decades.

She picked up a pebble and dropped it into the well, hearing a splash far below. "I said I'm expecting a baby."

"When?" he demanded, sounding thunderstruck.

She turned back to him. "I'm in the first trimester, when all the fun stuff like morning sickness is at its worst."

"Which explains your symptoms." He raked a hand through his hair, leaving trails. "Why did you let me think you had the flu?"

She scuffed the cobblestones with the toe of her shoe. "I didn't want you to think any less of me."

"Is my opinion so important to you?"

"So it would seem."

"Why, Cris?"

Because his kisses had inflamed the remnants of her teenage crush, and if she wasn't careful, she feared they could explode into something far more adult. The prospect scared the life out of her. Even if Eduard's royal position hadn't made a future with him impossible, she wasn't ready to risk her heart so soon after her experience with Mark. "I guess one rejection is enough for me at the moment." One admission, too.

Eduard planted one foot on the stone wall surrounding the terrace, and rested his forearm on his knee. "You're referring to the baby's father?"

She nodded. "My brother introduced us. Mark worked with Jeff in the money market. The first few times Mark asked me out, I turned him down. I'm not sure why. An instinct for self-preservation, most likely." Well-founded as it had turned out, she thought. "He kept asking until I agreed, and we saw one another for some months before my father died. He was even willing to move with me to Carramer. After Dad died, I felt so bereft that I turned to Mark for comfort."

"Which he was more than willing to provide," Eduard drawled.

Despite nerves stretched to breaking point, she managed a weak smile. She guessed that Eduard had read Mark more accurately in a few seconds than she had done in months. Was the ability to sum up people a trick of the royal trade? She wished she'd had the ability when she'd first met Mark, then she might not have been taken in by his shallow charm.

"I needed someone so badly," she went on, as much to herself as to him. "I didn't stop to think, to take any precautions, and by the time it occurred to Mark, it was too late. When I started to suspect I might be pregnant, it didn't seem to matter because I thought Mark would want the baby as much as I did."

Eduard came to her but kept a whisper of distance between them. Already the rejection was starting, she thought on a wave of pain. "I gather Lucas let you down," he said.

She laughed hollowly. "That's one way to describe it. When I told him I was expecting his child, he offered me money to…solve the problem, as he put it." Her voice broke on the last part.

Eduard grasped the edge of the wishing well with both hands, hard enough to loosen some of the mortar, she saw, as she heard it tumble into the depths. "Are you sure he didn't offer you the money to help defray your medical expenses?"

She clasped her arms around herself, knowing it was the only comfort she could expect now he knew the truth. "When Mark called me here a few days ago, he tried to convince me that's what he meant, but I know it wasn't."

"Perhaps he had a change of heart."

"Leopards don't change their spots that quickly."

The tremor she was unable to keep out of her voice made Eduard look at her in concern. "Don't worry, I'm not about to fall apart," she assured him. "I want this baby more than anything in the world, and I won't let Mark spoil things for me."

His mouth thinned. "Do you think he might try?"

"He told me he intends to come after me, although I warned him not to waste his time." She lifted a trembling hand to her face. "I guess I have you to thank for his sudden turnaround."

Shock made Eduard's features pale and he jammed his thumbs into his belt, to keep them away from her, she assumed, not sure if that was good or bad. She ached for his touch so badly that she swayed toward him before she got herself under control.

"Considering I've never met Lucas, you'd better explain my supposed influence on his behavior," Eduard ground out.

She didn't blame him for being angry. "That came out wrong. I only meant that Mark changed his mind after he found out from Jeff that I'm staying with a member of the royal family. According to Jeff, Mark's business is struggling. Knowing him, he probably hopes I can convince you to get involved in one of his deals.''

Irony suffused Eduard's expression. ''Scruples as well as honor, he sounds like quite a guy.''

''Go ahead, tell me what good taste I have in men.'' She let her tone tell him she was already well aware of it.

''You can't judge all men by the actions of one.''

''Can't I? You haven't exactly welcomed my news.'' She didn't add that she had dreaded his rejection most of all. His reluctance to come near her had confirmed her worst fears.

He straightened. ''If you must know, I'm stunned. Blind Freddie could tell that something was wrong with you, but I never suspected the real reason.''

She felt the urge to lash out, recognizing disappointment as the goad. ''Nothing is wrong with me. I'm having a baby, that's all. I shouldn't be surprised *you* don't understand, after being rejected by an expert.''

He moved so fast that he had pulled her against him before she had time to react. ''Does this feel like rejection to you?''

Her breathing had become so ragged that she felt light-headed, and she clung to him. ''No, it doesn't,'' she whispered hoarsely. It felt more like he intended to kiss her.

Eduard knew he was going to kiss her as soon as he saw her apprehensive expression, and realized she cared what he thought of her. He was still having difficulty coming to terms with her news. She wasn't a teenager any longer, but a mother-to-be. He let his breath whistle out as he struggled to make the mental leap.

She still looked like a girl, felt like one in his arms, he thought, feeling a surge of response he could barely control. Pressed against him, her stomach felt smooth under her jeans and skimpy shirt that revealed her tanned midriff. Nothing showed yet. But for her pallor and difficulty keeping food down in the mornings, he'd never have known.

Did she have any idea how worried he'd been? His mind had worked overtime on possibilities, although obviously never the right one. His hold on her tightened. She'd scared the devil out of him, worrying about what might be wrong with her. What that said about his feelings for her, he would need time to consider.

Right now he felt his spirits rise to giddy heights that he had to work to restrain, as he thought what her pregnancy might mean to him. The possibility was too new, too precarious for him to raise with her yet. First he had to convince her that rejecting her was the last thing he intended to do.

Telling himself the kiss was to reassure her, he almost laughed at the transparency of his motives. He had ached to taste her lips again since the night he followed her into the rain forest. Something he'd said had panicked her into walking away. Since then, he'd controlled the impulse to take her in his arms, although not without considerable effort.

He should probably resist the temptation now, considering her condition, and what she'd evidently been through with Lucas. But Eduard had always subscribed to the notion that the best way to resist temptation was to yield to it.

Under his hands, she quivered, making him wish he could don a suit of armor and take on the world as her champion. She didn't want protecting. She'd made that clear enough to Lucas as well. But a man could dream, couldn't he?

He felt as if he was dreaming now as he held her, the sight of her wide eyes, dark with uncertainty, playing havoc with his wish to be gentle.

He framed her face in both hands, feeling his breath become increasingly uneven. She licked her lips, the childlike gesture dissolving the last of his restraint. He had to taste her. He lowered his mouth to hers.

Her lips were still parted, still moist, offering no resistance when he kissed her. Deliberately he kept the kiss light, although everything in him wanted more, wanted to carry her inside and lose himself in her softness until they were both boneless with pleasure. Never before had he felt so driven by desire, so capable of taking what he wanted and never mind the consequences. But he wouldn't. The civilized part of him held the beast at bay, barely. Through the exquisite kiss, Eduard felt that primitive part of him battling the chains, demanding just this once…just this once.

''No.'' He wouldn't have been surprised if he'd spoken the denial out loud. This wasn't the way or the time. If he allowed himself to take advantage of her vulnerability for his own satisfaction, he was no better than the man who had given her a child then rejected them both.

The beast within him howled again, this time at the injustice of such treatment. If the child had been his, Eduard knew nothing on earth could have made him turn her away. He began to hope that Lucas would show his face here, for the simple pleasure of rearranging it for him.

What was it about Carissa that brought out such tendencies? Eduard didn't think of himself as a violent man. The navy had trained him in the killing arts, but he had hoped never to have to use them. Yet within a heartbeat of touching her, he was fighting the urge to possess her in the most primeval way, and relishing the thought of hurting the man who had hurt her.

Her pulse hammered under the fingers he slid over her face and throat. He cupped her face for an instant longer before releasing her, feeling the flame of desire slowly dampen and his breathing ease. The need for her still sang in his blood, but softly, a dull ache rather than a ravening demand.

Soon, he would make love to her, he promised himself. Not yet. Not while she still felt uncertain of him. He read it in her eyes, making him want to kill Lucas for what he'd done. Eduard's kiss had subdued some of her doubts, but there was still a way to go to convince her that she had nothing to fear from him.

She looked as shaken as he felt. "What happens now?" she asked, her voice not quite steady.

His wasn't much better. "I take you to Tricot to keep that appointment with Dr. Brunet."

"But I don't need…"

With his finger, he brushed away a smudge of dirt from her cheek, feeling his insides clench in response. This delicate woman was having a child. The instinct to care for her and her baby gripped him so hard, it was all he could do not to carry her off to the doctor then and there.

He shuddered at the thought of how he'd encouraged her to walk to the waterfall and to climb with him into the attic. If he'd harmed her or the child, however inadvertently, he would never forgive himself. "You need to take better care of yourself than you've been doing."

She gave an irritable shake of her head. "I'm pregnant, not incapacitated. Women have been having children for years while going about their normal lives."

He almost said, "They weren't having my baby" but of course, he didn't have that right. He settled for, "They didn't have me around."

She released a deep breath. "I won't have you around for much longer, either. So there's no point in wrapping me in cotton wool. I have to stand on my own feet sooner or later."

He heard what she didn't say, that Lucas had made her believe she had no other choice. One was slowly dawning on Eduard, but he didn't think now was the right time to raise it with her. "Humor me," he said. "Keep the appointment with Dr. Brunet and I'll treat you to lunch at Anini's." The restaurant was the perfect place for them to talk about the idea that increasingly held him in thrall.

Her eyebrows lifted. "Anini's is one of the most famous restaurants in the province." She had been surprised to see it was located in such an out-of-the-way place as Tricot, and had intended to treat herself to a celebratory meal there as soon as the lodge was up and running. Of course, that was before she lost most of her money to a con man. "I won't have you feeling sorry for me," she said, suspicion coloring her tone.

"You've guessed my hidden agenda," he said, the teasing note in his voice taking the wind out of her sails. "I take all my charity cases there." He tilted her chin with one finger. "I always eat there when I'm in town. If I go anywhere else, Anton Anini will think he's lost royal favor and slash his wrists."

"I wouldn't want to be responsible for anything like that," she said with mock seriousness, her eyes sparkling. His acceptance had given her a great gift, she knew. She had braced herself for him to react the way Mark and her brother had done, but Eduard had surprised her.

She shouldn't be surprised, she told herself. He had always been different. While his brother, Mathiaz, had awed her with his royal dignity, Eduard had been approachable, willing to listen to her concerns and share her dreams. No wonder she had convinced herself she was in love with him. Now, his concern made her feel cherished, something she'd definitely been lacking of late. This time she would be careful not to misread his response as anything more, she resolved.

Eduard offered to take her to Tricot in the helicopter but she declined, preferring the compact car she'd bought when she arrived to riding in the alarmingly small acrylic bubble.

"My stomach couldn't handle flying, even if my nerves could," she assured him.

He was equally unappreciative of her car, but insisted on driving. Even with the seat pushed back as far as it would go, he barely fitted behind the wheel.

The road to Tricot wound through forests of tropical and endangered plants that Eduard explained belonged to the Royal National Parks Authority. The gardens had been established to protect and restore some of Carramer's oldest plant species.

Beyond the plantation, the drive paralleled the Tiga River, the banks crowded with banana trees, bamboo thickets and stands of wild ginger. Snow-white egrets, night herons and rare Carramer waterbirds resided in the valley. Occasionally she caught a glimpse of the scarlet plumage of the Ramer parrot, the kingdom's bird emblem.

"Originally, this road was an ancient path that wound down to the riverbed," Eduard said, adopting the tone of a tour guide. "In the eighteen hundreds, the path became a horse trail, then a cobblestone carriage road. My forebears were fond of slipping away from Chateau Valmont to this cooler retreat."

The scenery was breathtaking, and the narrow, winding road suggested care, but surely not as much as Eduard was taking. Was he worried about the car holding together? "Aren't we going rather slowly?"

He kept his gaze on the road. "I don't want to shake you up too much."

Her sigh of exasperation exploded between them. "There's no need to treat me like glass. I promise I won't break into little pieces."

His look said she understood him too well. "I'll try to keep it in mind." He sped up, although not much, and she resigned herself to a leisurely journey to the town.

With its royal patronage, the area had become a fashionable place for the province's well-to-do to establish their own holiday ranches. As a result, although Tricot had only a few thousand permanent residents, the town was a stylish center of beautifully maintained old buildings and galleries showing the work of local artisans. The thriving tourist trade was the reason why she had thought the vicinity ideal for a bed-and-breakfast place.

Dr. Brunet's surgery was located in a restored timber house standing a few doors away from the Monarch Hotel, at one end of the main street. Bougainvillea twining around the veranda posts added a splash of brightness to the weathered exterior. "I'll be fine from here,'' she said as Eduard moved with her toward the building. She could imagine the rumors that would start flying if he insisted on escorting her in to see the doctor.

He nodded in reluctant agreement, and turned back to the car. ''I'll come back for you in half an hour.''

As soon as Carissa approached the reception area and identified herself, a petite, dark-haired local beauty in her late twenties jumped to her feet. ''Dr. Brunet is expecting you. You can go straight in.''

The waiting room held half a dozen people and Carissa felt uncomfortable at the obviously preferential treatment. She was sure it wouldn't have bothered Eduard. He was probably used to being given priority. Again, Carissa felt conscious of the gulf between them. In the isolation of the lodge, she had been less aware of his royal status. Seeing the way people reacted to him in the town made it harder to overlook.

As soon as he helped her out of the car, she had heard the murmured greetings, seen the heads bob in deference, and also noted the curiosity her presence aroused. She contrasted today with her first visit to Tricot to buy supplies soon after she moved into the lodge. No one had given her a second glance.

The doctor's manner had changed toward her as well, she noticed. This time he was far more solicitous of her welfare, and didn't chide her for choosing to live in an isolated location in her present condition. Being a friend of the marquis had its advantages, she decided.

She returned to the car to find Eduard leaning against it, his arms folded and a look of concern on his face. ''The doctor prescribed an iron supplement for me, but otherwise everything's fine,'' she told him. His look of relief suggested that he was glad she was well enough to be on her way.

It was time anyway, she decided. She couldn't impose on him for much longer. After lunch she would visit the local real estate office and see if there was anything available to rent within her budget. The thought was surprisingly unappealing.

As he had promised, Eduard took her to Anini's, the building reminding Carissa of an old plantation house from the American South, with a columned porch, high ceilings and louvred windows to catch the breeze.

Again, Eduard's royal status worked its magic. As Eduard had anticipated, the owner, Anton, personally escorted them to a table in the center of a covered terrace at the back of the building, looking onto a vista of mature trees draped with hanging vines and surrounded by impatiens, angel's trumpet plants and the vivid teacup-sized flowers of the golden-cup bush.

Beyond the garden, the river sparkled in the sunlight. A narrow path wound along the bank, little used except for the occasional jogger or dog walker, she noticed.

She gave a sigh of pleasure. "This is lovely."

Without taking his eyes off her, he murmured, "Lovely."

She couldn't fool herself that they were two ordinary people on a date, but she felt a tingle suffuse her. If she hadn't known better, she could easily have mistaken his frankly admiring gaze for that of a lover.

Wishful thinking, she told herself. Men often treated women differently once they knew they were pregnant. Eduard wouldn't have driven here at a snail's pace, nor would he look at her as if she were the eighth wonder of the world if not for her condition.

Conscious of her color heightening, she buried her

face in the extensive leather-bound menu, but finally gave up and closed it. Eduard raised an eyebrow at her. "You're not going to tell me you're not hungry."

"I'm not..." she began.

He gestured for Anton, who came to his side at once. "We'll go with your recommendations." He glanced back to Carissa.

A soft smile spread across the man's florid face. "It will be my pleasure to create a meal you will not easily forget," he said with a bow, and left them.

She refused Anton's offer of wine in favor of iced water. Eduard chose the same. He sipped it before saying, "Are you sure you're all right? Both of you?"

Unconsciously she crossed her hands over her stomach. "We're doing really well."

He frowned. "Then why were you so ill?"

"Dr. Brunet says it's nature's way of making sure new mothers don't gain too much weight too soon." She grimaced. "Although I would wish for a more pleasant solution. The doctor promised me things will improve in the next couple of months."

"They would want to."

He sounded so fierce that she laughed. How different he was from Mark, who had behaved as if the baby was an inconvenience. For a moment, she wished...no. She put a lid firmly on the thought. Eduard was only being kind, as was his nature. Once in her life was enough to misread his kindness. She was a lot older and wiser now.

Anton excelled himself with a meal consisting of a variety of Asian delicacies to start, followed by truffled mushroom pie, roasted quail with coconut rice, stir-fried ocean trout and an asparagus and cashew salad, arranging the dishes so they could both sample a little of everything.

By the time he brought the dessert, she felt as if she would burst. "No, really, I couldn't manage another bite."

"The raspberry soufflé is Anton's specialty," Eduard said.

It was such a refreshing change to enjoy her food that she weakened. "I know I'll regret this, but okay."

The owner looked vindicated as he refreshed their water glasses. When he left, Carissa looked around, realizing belatedly that they had the terrace area to themselves, although the main part of the restaurant buzzed with activity. She sipped her water then asked, "Does Anton always clear the decks for you?"

Eduard's gaze became hooded briefly. "I don't always allow it. I requested privacy now because there's something I want to ask you."

Here it comes, she thought, aware of a sweeping sense of disappointment. She should have known he had taken her news too well. Now he was about to ask her to leave before her condition became common knowledge. She had expected it, so why did she feel so disconsolate?

Her eyes brimmed and she blinked hard, looking toward the river while she fought to keep composure. She would not, repeat not, break down in front of Eduard. None of this was his fault. She should be thankful that he had allowed her to remain at the lodge this long.

"I know what you're going to say," she said when she could trust her voice. "I intend to start looking for a new place to live this afternoon."

Her quick glance at him revealed a look of puzzlement. "A new place? Cris, that wasn't…"

Suddenly she put a hand on his arm. "Look, down there."

He followed her gaze. "The man walking beside the river? Sorry, I don't recognize him."

Her fingers tightened on his arm. "I do. I'm sure it's Dominic Hass, the man who tried to sell me the lodge."

Chapter Eight

Eduard didn't hesitate. Springing to his feet, he dropped a platinum credit card on the table and snagged the attention of a passing waiter to give Anton the message that he'd been called away unexpectedly. "Hass can't have gone far."

The thought of the marquis confronting the con man brought her heart into her throat. "Shouldn't we contact the police?"

"I don't want to give your friend time to disappear again. I'll call the law as soon as I find out where Hass is headed."

If Eduard thought he was leaving her at the restaurant, she had news for him. "I'm coming with you."

He gave an emphatic shake of his head. "Not in your condition."

Not in any condition, she heard in his tone. His desire to protect her was admirable, but misplaced. This was her fight and he wasn't leaving her out of it. "I'm pregnant, not feeble. You only caught a glimpse of Hass. You need me to identify him.''

Eduard gave her a look of frustration. ''Unfortunately you're right, but I want you to promise you won't take any unnecessary risks.''

She could see he wasn't budging without the assurance. And he hadn't said anything about necessary risks. ''Agreed.''

A staircase led directly off the terrace down to the river walk. By the time they reached the water there was no sign of Dominic Hass. The path ended at a thick stand of trees reaching down to the riverbank. Carissa looked around uncertainly.

Eduard followed the line of her gaze to the trees. ''He was heading in that direction when you saw him. He could be hiding out in the trees.''

She nodded. ''When I arrived in Tricot, I drove past a group of cabins on the other side of these woods. Could Hass be staying there?''

Eduard looked thoughtful. ''It makes as much sense as him remaining in the area in the first place.''

She had been thinking the same thing. ''Maybe he's looking for new victims for his tricks.''

''Unlikely. Once his kind find their mark, they usually head for greener—and safer—pastures. Sticking around offers too much chance of being caught.''

The mystery of why Hass had stayed in Tricot would only be solved when they caught up with him. Seeing Eduard's determination to do just that, Carissa quickened her steps to keep up with him.

When the trees closed around them, he moved more cautiously, taking her hand to keep her close. The green canopy filtered out most of the sunlight, and she shivered in the sudden coolness, glad of Eduard's comforting grip. A carpet of fallen leaves muffled their steps. Amid the looming shadows, she half expected the con man to be lying in wait for them behind the next tree.

Hass didn't know she'd seen him, she reminded herself, wondering if the sighting owed more to wishful thinking than reality. She paused, earning a questioning look from Eduard. "Is something the matter?"

She chewed her lower lip. "Maybe the man I saw only looked like Hass."

The marquis's eyebrows lifted. "Getting cold feet?"

"You said yourself it makes little sense for him still to be in the vicinity."

He folded his arms and rested his back against a tree, enjoying having her to himself in such a primitive setting. Her eyes were wide with doubts and her hair was mussed where a tree branch had caught it. His wish to catch up with Hass for her sake didn't prevent him from appreciating how beautiful she looked. "Only one way to find out," he said.

She tugged at a twig caught in her hair. "Are you always so single-minded?"

He reached to remove the twig for her, enjoying the feel of his fingers tangling briefly in the silken strands of her hair. Wanting to cup her head and bring her lips to his, he settled for brushing the hair away from her eyes. "Always."

"I could have been mistaken."

He heard the tremor in her voice that his touch had put there. "We both know you weren't."

Her long lashes swept down. "How can you be sure?"

"When we were younger, if someone moved or changed something around, you were usually the first to notice and comment on it," he said. "If you think you saw Hass, that's good enough for me."

Her tentative smile made Eduard glad he had remembered her acute powers of observation. He remembered lots more. The way her hair strayed into her eyes, needing the brush of a hand to subdue it, and the way her eyes filmed when something touched her deeply.

It happened now, making him ache to take her into his arms and kiss the uncertainty away. Not sure he would be able to stop at comforting her, he resisted the inclination. The best thing he could do for her right now was find her con man and get her nest egg back for her or, if that wasn't possible, give her the satisfaction of seeing the man brought to justice.

With a sigh, Eduard set off through the trees again.

The trees gave way to a pleasant area of parkland equipped with a stone barbecue and timber table and benches. A low stone fence divided the park from the cluster of cabins Carissa had noticed. A sign welcomed visitors to the Rain Forest Resort. Beside the sign, a gate stood open.

Carissa froze. "There's Hass, walking around the side of the main building. He must have rented a cabin around the back. Now we know where to find him we can call the police."

The marquis's sharp gesture stayed her. "First I want to make sure we have the right man."

"You said you trust my judgment."

His expression turned stony. "It isn't a question of trust. I don't fancy the headlines were I to order the arrest of the wrong man."

For a minute she had allowed herself to forget. Eduard wasn't like other men. As a member of the royal family, any mistakes he made would be broadcast far and wide. She nibbled on a fingernail. "I keep forgetting."

He favored her with a wry grin. "One of the things I like about you."

Buoyed up by the near-compliment, she squared her shoulders. "Maybe if we phone in an anonymous tip-off…?"

"By the time the police decide it isn't a hoax, Hass could be long gone. We'll handle this ourselves for now."

At least Eduard was no longer trying to shut her out, she thought in satisfaction. Not that it would have done any good. In spite of the misgivings she had expressed to Eduard, she was sure the man she had seen was Hass, and she wanted to talk to him so badly she could taste it. Her money was probably a lost cause, no doubt sent well away from Carramer by now, but she could still see Hass himself in jail.

"You'd better stay out of sight while I find out which cabin he's using," Eduard suggested. As she opened her mouth to protest, he added, "We don't want to risk having him recognize you and take off."

She could say the same about him, but she kept behind Eduard as he rounded the building to where a row of cabins stood in beautifully landscaped gardens beside a kidney-shaped swimming pool. Motioning her to keep back, he made his way along the row, checking each cabin in turn. At this time of the day most of the occupants were out, but she saw him tense as he reached the last cabin in the row. He rapped on the door and called out, "Room service."

The door inched open and she ducked behind a parked car. She heard a man's voice start to say, "I didn't order any—"

Before he could finish the sentence, the door rocked on its hinges as Eduard slammed it against the wall and forced his way in.

By the time she got there, the marquis had Hass's arms locked behind his back. Over his shoulder, Eduard said, "Looks like we've found your man."

Ice water skidded down her spine. "That's him." The man's face was bruised, but not from anything Eduard had done. In contrast to his prisoner, the marquis wasn't even breathing hard.

"How did you know?" she asked a heartbeat later as it dawned on her that he hadn't waited for her to identify Hass before immobilizing the man.

Eduard looked grim. "As soon as he saw me, he tried to make a fast exit through the bedroom window. It was as good as a confession."

Hass squirmed, his expression growing desperate. She guessed that every move caused pain to shoot along his arm from Eduard's implacable grip. "I don't know what you're talking about," he yelped.

"Then you didn't con this young lady into buying an estate belonging to me?"

Sweat beaded the captive's brow. "How could I? I have no idea who you are."

Carissa stepped forward. "Mr. Hass, it's time you were introduced to Commander Eduard de Marigny, Marquis of Merrisand, the rightful owner of Tiga Falls Lodge."

Eduard cut off Hass's profane response by jerking his arm higher. "One more word and I'll break it for you," the marquis vowed. Carissa didn't doubt he was capable of carrying out the threat.

Hass seemed to sense it, too, and stopped swearing. He sagged in Eduard's grasp, the fight ebbing out of him as he said, "If you want to hurt me, you'll have to join the queue."

"What does he mean?" Carissa asked.

"You're probably not the only one after his blood. Right, Hass?"

The man swallowed audibly. "Right, unfortunately. Only he threatened to come back with some friends and kill me."

"Who's he?"

Hass's gaze darted helplessly around the cabin. "The man I sold the lodge to a few days ago."

Carissa crossed her arms. "You mean you pulled the same trick on someone else after me?"

Hass tried to pull away. "It's not my fault there's a shortage of good properties."

Eduard exerted pressure on the man's arm, eliciting a howl of protest that made Carissa wince in sympathy. "If things are getting so hot for you around here, why did you stick around?"

"I had no choice. My vic...my client snatched my wallet and passport. You can't trust anybody these days."

So the con man had been conned by one of his own victims. If Hass hadn't caused such havoc in her life, she would have laughed.

Eduard shoved Hass across the room so he landed on a couch, winded and pale. Looming over him, the marquis demanded, "The papers were probably forged anyway. What happened to the money you took from Miss Day?"

Carissa held her breath as Hass cringed away, his eyes round with fear. "A deposit slip for her check was in my wallet. Without any ID, I couldn't get at it.

I don't have a bean right now, or I'd be miles away from here by now.''

So that was that. She hadn't realized how much she had been counting on Hass still having her nest egg in his possession. The slender hope slipped away, and she felt her shoulders slump. Then she straightened. At least Hass hadn't gotten away with his crime, thanks to Eduard.

"Once the owner of this place knows I've been cleaned out, I'll be out on my ear," Hass whined.

"I'll be glad to arrange alternative accommodation for you," Eduard said. "It won't be as fancy as this, but I guarantee it's a lot more secure."

The con man lifted his hands in surrender. "It's an improvement on watching my back every minute."

Eduard nodded agreement. "However tempted I am to leave you to your just desserts, I won't." To Carissa, he said, "Call the police."

She used the cabin's telephone to do so, finding once again that invoking Eduard's name produced almost instantaneous results. The officer who arrived a short time later was the soul of deference, obviously pleased to be of service to the marquis.

With Hass handcuffed and locked in the back of the police car, the officer returned to take their statements. When Carissa's voice faltered as she explained how she had been conned, Eduard's look of support made it easier for her to admit the embarrassing details.

"You're not his first victim, but thanks to you and Lord Merrisand, you might be his last," the officer said, closing his notebook and standing up. "My superiors are delighted to have Hass in custody. I contacted them after your phone call, and they told me they have a file on him thicker than the phone book. They're sending a detective to escort him to Perla.''

It was some consolation, Carissa thought. She couldn't bring herself to ask the officer if there was any chance she would see her money again.

Eduard anticipated her question. ''The man who stole Hass's papers threatened to return with some friends.''

The officer's eyes gleamed. ''Don't worry, Lord Merrisand, if they show up, I'll have people waiting for them.''

''I'd like to be kept informed.''

The statement was phrased in a polite but unmistakable tone of command. The officer came to automatic attention. ''I'll be in touch as soon as we know anything more, sir. And Miss Day, if we can get your money back, rest assured we will.''

She didn't allow herself to hope too much as she murmured her thanks.

Carissa looked all in, Eduard thought. Not surprising. This experience was enough to drain anyone, far less someone in her condition. He made her sit down on a chair beside the pool while they waited for the officer to arrange with the manager of the resort to keep Hass's cabin locked until it could be properly searched.

When the officer came back, Eduard declined his offer of a police driver to return them to the lodge. ''I'd appreciate it if someone can collect Miss Day's car and bring it here,'' he said. ''We're staying in Tricot tonight.''

Aware of Carissa's look of surprise, he didn't elaborate until the officer had driven off with Hass glowering in the back. ''After all that's happened, I'm not subjecting you to another trip over those back roads today.''

''I'm fine,'' she insisted, her assertion contradicted by the tiredness he heard in her voice.

She looked fine. Better than fine, gorgeous. Before leaving the lodge this morning she had changed into a finely woven overshirt in a swirly pattern of lemon and lime over wide-legged pants of the same material. Her feet were encased in leather sandals, the total effect making her seem younger than her years.

He watched her comb her hair with her fingers. ''I don't have anything with me for an overnight stay.''

''This may be a small place, but I'm sure we can find you a toothbrush somewhere.''

She shot him a look of exasperation. ''What about a change of clothes? Really, I don't mind driving back.''

His expression said the subject was closed. ''Not on my watch.''

''And what you say goes, my lord.'' She gave the title almost insulting emphasis and started to pace.

He smiled, enjoying her graceful movements. He wondered if she was aware that the sun behind her made her clothes translucent. ''Now you're getting the idea.''

Her jaw set into a mutinous line, making him want to erase the moodiness with a kiss. He restrained himself, well aware that his decision to remain in Tricot overnight was going to cost him. Like it or not, he'd been brought up a gentleman. That meant separate bedrooms and a hands-off policy until she made it clear she wanted something different.

Not that he couldn't try to convince her to want

something more, he thought with an inner smile. "Where would you like to stay?" he asked.

Her eyes flashed fire at him. "I wouldn't presume to interfere with your plans for me."

He couldn't help it. He tipped her under the chin. "You sulk beautifully, you know."

He didn't like the way she shied away from his hand. "If you say so, my lord."

He folded his arms. "How about dropping this title stuff right now?"

"Or you'll do what? Have me thrown into a cell beside Hass?"

Better, he thought. At least she was responding to him, although not in a way he cared for. "Have you ever heard of lèse-majesté?" he asked mildly.

"It means treason against the crown," she snapped. "I studied French at school."

"In Carramer, lèse-majesté is more than an abstract concept."

His warning tone raised her eyebrows. "You mean it's a crime against the crown not to bow and scrape before your royal wonderfulness?"

He felt his mouth twitch, negating the severe look he was trying for. "I guess I asked for that. Just as you're asking for this."

Taking her by the shoulders, he lowered his mouth to hers, kissing her long and deeply. He felt the instant when her resistance faltered and her lips parted to welcome him. In that moment he was no longer a royal figure on a pedestal, but a man with needs and desires that she stirred within him as no other woman had done.

Reluctantly he lifted his mouth from hers, becoming aware of where they were. But the pool area remained deserted, the other cabins quiet. No one had seen his lapse of discretion. Lapse, nothing, he told himself. He had done exactly what he wanted to do.

She looked dreamy, as if held in thrall by his kiss. Dare he hope that she felt some of the magic that infused him whenever he touched her? She gave a half shake of her head, as if denying the hope. "I think we should go back."

He heard her uncertainty as a confession. She was no more sure of herself than he was around her. The night ahead began to seem more promising.

He buried the sudden rush of anticipation under a wry grin. "We could stay right here. We know there's at least one unoccupied cabin."

There would be one for him anyway. He had only to ask and the world fell into step with his wishes. The anger in the thought gave her pause. What was really bothering her? The influence he wielded so easily, or the way he affected her so strongly?

She had no reason to make an issue of his status now. He had been titled as long as she'd known him, and it had never troubled her before. But she had felt no need of a buffer between them until now.

"On the other hand, I don't want you anywhere near here if Hass's friends come calling," Eduard continued.

She'd forgotten about them. Eduard had made her forget. He was good at doing that. Too good, she thought, troubled at how few defenses she had against him. Blaming her sensitivity on her pregnancy didn't fully explain the way she melted at his slightest touch.

She had never felt this way with Mark. If not for the baby, she would never have considered marrying him. Perhaps she had sensed that he had a darker side, although he had disguised it well until she told him she was pregnant.

In the lonely time following her father's death, she had needed Mark. She wanted Eduard. It was as simple as that.

All the more reason to insist that they return to the lodge tonight.

She might as well have saved her breath. A young police officer arrived with her car, treating it like a limousine instead of cheap transportation. If he wondered what the marquis was doing in such a rattletrap, he didn't show it as he took up a post in front of Hass's cabin.

Eduard listened gravely to her arguments then settled her in the front seat, and drove back toward the main street as he'd intended to do all along.

She had expected him to take her to the Monarch Hotel, the only accommodation available in Tricot other than the cabins they had just left. But Eduard parked outside Anini's. She frowned. "What are we doing here?"

"Anton keeps a riverfront suite that he makes available to friends. It's popular with honeymooners," he explained. "I've borrowed it on occasion, although not for that purpose. I think you'll like it."

Naturally the suite was available, and of course the marquis and his companion were welcome to the use of it for as many nights as they desired. Anton would be delighted to send in a special dinner as soon as they wished.

"Why aren't I surprised?" she murmured.

Set a little apart from the main building, the suite was lavishly appointed, with two spacious bedrooms, each with its own bathroom, and an open-plan sitting and dining room. French doors opened onto a full-length terrace complete with hot tub and a view across the river to the green-clad hills. "Where does the spiral staircase lead?" she asked, too tired to explore further for now.

"To a tower with a telescope for admiring the view," he explained. "While I'm gone, you can choose which bedroom you prefer."

"Where are you going?"

"Toothbrushes, remember?"

Before she could remind him that she needed more than a toothbrush if she was to spend a comfortable night here, the door closed behind him. She tossed a mental coin and chose the bedroom on the right.

A roomy four-poster responded to her test bounce with satisfying resilience. A fluffy white bathrobe with the tags still attached hung behind the door. The bathroom, with corner bathtub, yielded a selection of toiletries worthy of a five-star hotel. Even a toothbrush, she noticed with a smile. Eduard could have skipped his shopping expedition.

The smile faded as she imagined sharing the suite with him. It seemed a thousand times more intimate than the lodge. He'd called it a honeymoon suite and that was what it felt like as she stretched out on the bed.

Tired as she was, she couldn't make herself relax, knowing not only was this *not* a honeymoon, but it never would be as long as she and Eduard remained worlds apart.

Chapter Nine

"What's all this?" she asked when he returned with packages that he piled on the coffee table in the sitting room. "You went out to buy toothbrushes."

He looked insufferably pleased with himself. "I got carried away."

"You're not kidding." At his urging she began to open boxes. The first held a nightdress in opalescent silk trimmed with French lace. A matching peignoir nestled in tissue in the second box.

When she lifted the nightdress out, it cascaded over her hands like foam. A quick vision of herself wearing it for him brought color surging into her face. "I can't possibly accept this."

She saw a light come into his eyes. "You could leave it off altogether. I don't mind."

She slapped away the hand he reached out to her. "If that's my only other choice, I'll wear the clothes. But I insist on repaying you." As befitted a fashionable retreat, Tricot's shops were lovely but expensive. She would be quite a while paying for these, she suspected.

She picked up the smallest package and shook it with no effect. "What's this?"

He grinned. "I promised you a toothbrush."

Curious in spite of herself, she opened the wrapping to reveal a filigree glass holder containing a toothbrush fashioned in the shape of a tiger. Snuggled alongside it was a baby-sized toothbrush with downy bristles, designed like the tiger's cub. Her heart turned over.

"You do realize babies don't have teeth for a long time," she said, her voice betrayingly husky.

He smiled. "You have to admit, it's cute."

Eduard would be the kind of father who bought a train set while his son was still in the cradle, she thought. He would play with the train himself, having convinced himself that he was getting the hang of it for the baby's sake.

So why did he react so badly when she talked about him having children of his own? Something was wrong here, but she was too emotionally fragile to puzzle it out. She settled for thanking him as she folded the wrappings.

His expression turned sheepish. "I also remembered what you said about needing a change of clothes." From behind his back he produced a carrier bag from a boutique whose window display Carissa had admired. The lack of price tags on the lovely things on show had deterred her from going in.

In the carrier was a T-shirt she had admired in the window. It was white with an intricate design based on the ancient Carramer symbols called Mayati, turtles in this case. She held it against herself. He had judged the size perfectly. "It's gorgeous. Do the symbols have a meaning?"

He nodded. "To the Mayat people, the turtle symbolized the blessing of children."

She went to him, grasping his arm. Under her hand, she felt padded muscle. The urge to keep touching was almost overwhelming. "Thank you for the gifts, and for being so accepting. Your friendship and support means a lot to me." The acceptance more than the gifts, she knew.

"I shall always be your friend, Cris."

Something in his tone made her breath catch as she arrived at her own interpretation. Was he telling her that in spite of the gifts and the tension clogging the atmosphere between them, that was all they could be to each other?

He walked out onto the terrace. She followed him, finding him watching the river. The setting sun washed the sandstone paving and stone balustrade with golden light. Below them, the river was a strand of diamonds, spilling across the landscape. The path beside it was deserted, birdsong the only sound to be heard.

Uncertainty made a taut knot inside her. "It must be hell being born with a title, always having to live for duty rather than desire."

He shifted to look at her. "Is that what you think I'm doing?"

She barely heard him. She had hoped for more than friendship from him, despite her pregnancy putting paid to any such dream. In her heart still lived the foolish teenager who had fallen in love with him, she discovered. Well, it was time for her to grow up. She spread her hands. "What else can I think? You're royal and I'm not, so even if I wasn't having a baby, we can never be more than friends.''

''You could be a lot more to me, Cris.''

His statement caught her by surprise, along with the swift move that brought him to her side. He found her hands. Clasping them in one of his, he lifted them to his lips.

His mouth scorched where it touched, and a shiver rippled through her. ''You're confusing me.''

He caught a strand of her hair around his finger. ''It's only fair, considering what you do to me.''

She hadn't expected that, any more than she had expected to find herself close enough to feel his breath whispering against her cheek. She felt lost, unable to interpret his change of mood. ''You'll have to explain. I'm having trouble keeping up.''

''You're not the only one.'' Irresistibly drawn, he bent his head and brushed her lips, the sweet taste of her making nonsense of his intention to remain aloof.

It wasn't fair to let her think his title was the reason he needed to keep his emotional distance. Knowing he couldn't give her children, he had no right to touch her, far less drink as deeply of her warm, mobile mouth as he was doing.

He hadn't suggested spending the night here in order to seduce her; at least, he didn't think he had. Sharing the lodge, he'd had no trouble keeping to his own room at night. So why was he letting the change of scene undermine his resolve?

He wasn't being fully honest with himself, he knew. Remaining in his bed alone, night after night, knowing she was nearby, had taken every ounce of self-discipline he possessed. He had stayed away because it was the right thing—the only thing—to do.

What was different now?

She was pregnant, that was the difference. For the first time since the doctors had shattered his future with their news, he dared to hope. Whether the hope was justified would depend on Carissa.

Telling her the truth and letting her give him her answer was the noble thing to do. How much easier it was to be noble when she was several rooms away. Now in his arms, her softness and warmth were too alluring. He would have had to be a true hero to resist.

He wasn't that heroic. A title and a royal lineage were no protection from the urge to taste all she was, and show her all the tenderness he could, before he sent her to her own bed, alone.

Knowing he couldn't, in good conscience, do more until she had thought through the proposition he wanted to place before her, he reined in his runaway feelings, and focused on giving her everything that was within his power.

As he let his hands wander where they would, caressing, touching, teasing, he felt the frantic beat of the pulse at her throat and bent to kiss the spot. She let her head drop back, her breathing quickening. He saw her struggle to absorb the sensations pouring through her. She was a heartbeat from surrendering to him.

Yearnings he could barely name gripped him with feverish intensity, making him distrust that he could master himself sufficiently to give her this without taking more. The need was there, achingly powerful, threatening to drag them both past the point of no return.

How could she have thought herself loved before? Carissa wondered. Nothing she had experienced or imagined compared with the blaze of Eduard's lips against her skin, the searing touch of his hands, the taste of him on her tongue.

Her nipples hardened against her shirt and she arched against him, desperate for more closeness, telling him with every swaying movement that nothing he wanted from her could possibly be wrong.

Was she in love with Eduard? Had she ever *not* been in love with him? The questions clamored at her fogged mind, and she let herself touch him as if physical contact would provide her with answers. She should have known that wasn't the way. All she did was drive herself closer to the brink.

His control hung by a thread, she sensed. She could feel his heart thundering against her chest and his eyes looked almost black, the pupils like stars in a night sky. What was holding him back? He'd assured her it wasn't the baby. So what was the matter?

With a shuddering sigh, she found her voice. "I feel as if there's a wall between us."

His lips moved against her hairline, the intimate gesture making nonsense of her claim. "Does this feel like a wall to you?"

Wanting to believe him, she couldn't make the leap. "There is something. I can feel it."

He lifted his head and released a sharp breath. "Yes."

"Isn't it time you shared it with me?" Until he did, she would go on fearing that she was the problem. Everything in her hungered to go on and on until they toppled over the brink together, but without openness and trust, she couldn't risk it.

He felt her tension grow, and let his mouth brush her lips a final time before releasing her. She prowled to the parapet and leaned against it, the evening breeze ruffling her hair. She was so slight, so graceful. She looked as if the breeze might waft her away. But as he had held her, he had felt her core of strength. She would need it to deal with what he was about to say next.

"I want you to marry me," he said softly.

She spun around, her eyes wide. "What?"

The play of evening light on her features made her look so ethereal that he ached for her. Until she knew everything, he wouldn't allow himself to take any more than he had already done, which was already more than he was entitled to, in truth.

It didn't stop him wanting more.

"I was going to propose to you at Anini's, but then you spotted Hass," he went on.

Bewilderment clouded her lovely features. He understood why. After telling her he wanted to remain her friend, the last thing she would have expected was a proposal of marriage.

Wanting to give her time to absorb his intentions for them, he took her hands and led her to a banquette that edged one side of the terrace. She looked impatient as he settled her there, but curbed the questions that had to be rioting through her mind. "Before you give me your answer, there's something you need to know," he said.

Knowing that her patience must come at a price, he decided not to try it too far, although he was impressed by her steadiness. The perfect royal bride indeed. He took a deep breath. "At the lodge, you asked me about the sea rescue I was involved in."

She nodded, looking distracted. "I gather you don't like talking about it."

"And you wondered why?"

"I thought…an excess of modesty. I saw your face when I called you a hero, although the families of the people you rescued weren't in any doubt."

He let his eyes close briefly, then opened them to her sweetly puzzled expression. She still didn't understand what this had to do with his proposal of marriage. He hunted for the words to explain it to her, wishing briefly that her condition didn't rule out alcohol. Reluctant to indulge alone, he couldn't rely on a stiff drink to make this easier. He was probably better keeping a clear head anyway. "I have no regrets about what I did that day. Given the same conditions, I'd do exactly what I did before. But there were consequences."

She paled. As soon as she had seen Eduard's name linked with the event, she had followed the reports of the rescue compulsively. "The news reports didn't say anything about you being injured." Was that why he had disappeared from view right after the event?

He shook his head. "I wasn't, not in the way you mean."

"Then what?" On a rush of realization, she said, "The chemicals leaking into the sea?" Her hand found his, and she held tight.

"They were highly toxic to humans," he said, his grip firming in hers. "I can't say I wasn't warned before I went in."

"You went anyway."

"Lives were at stake."

It was said in the manner of "anyone would have done the same," but she seriously doubted it. "You said there were consequences. What happened?"

"I spent some time in the hospital, letting my family use their influence to keep it from the world media. Like you, the media blamed my reticence on an excess

of modesty." His mouth curved into a humorless smile.
"Better that than the truth, which was that the exposure
left me physically unharmed, but destroyed any chance
that I can ever father children."

She couldn't hide her shock, or the compassion that
overtook it for what he had sacrificed. Such a price
was beyond imagining, yet it was so easy to imagine
him willingly paying it to save lives. She felt chagrined
for mentioning children to him so casually, without
knowing what she was putting him through.

He obviously wanted children, so the loss of such a
possibility must be a cruel blow. "I'm sorry," she said,
wishing she could think of a more meaningful response.

"It could have been worse." The lightness he in-
jected into his tone didn't quite reach his eyes. "I assure you I'm still a man in every other way that mat-
ters."

Her blush told him she had worked that out for herself. She would have to be made of stone not to be
aware of her effect on him, and of the iron control that
had enabled him to stop at kissing her.

Had he not, she doubted if she would have been as
strong.

He stood up and walked to the hot tub, staring into
the water. "After I found out what had happened, I
promised myself I would never marry and deprive my
partner of her own child."

Yet he had just proposed to her. "The baby," she
said, conscious of a dragging ache setting up somewhere in the region of her heart. "That's what this is
all about, isn't it?"

He turned to her, casting a shadow across her, as if
his words hadn't done that already. The enormity of

what he wanted from her took her breath away, but not with passion, this time. His news had burned away what remained of that, although the embers smoldered inside, where she knew they would take a long time to go out.

He wanted to marry her, not because he loved her, but because she could give him the child he wanted, and he wouldn't have to feel guilty for depriving her of the chance at motherhood.

Oblivious to her churning emotions, he said, "I care about you a great deal, Cris. I would deem it a privilege if you would agree to be my wife and let me be a father to your child."

Honorable to the last, she thought, her anger mounting. She stood, barely able to control her shaking. "I hadn't realized my pregnancy would prove so convenient." To think she had agonized about telling him, for fear of disappointing him. He hadn't had any such qualms where she was concerned.

His expression showed genuine confusion. "I'm thinking of you, too."

She couldn't stand it if he offered her pity. He didn't need to think he was doing her a favor with his offer. "Oh, please. Don't make this worse than it already is."

She had surprised him, she saw. "You have to admit, it is a workable solution for both of us," he said mildly.

She let her eyes blaze her fury at him. If there had been any justice, he would have been incinerated where he stood. Instead, he looked back at her with that luminous gaze that had made her feel so feminine and desirable such a short time ago. She felt the effect starting now, and drove it back with anger. "Don't you think I might want more from marriage than a workable solution? Or don't you think pregnant single women have that right?'' According to her brother, they didn't. He would expect her to be grateful that Eduard was willing to marry her as she was.

She didn't feel grateful. She felt cheated. Eduard had aroused her as no man had ever done, making her feel as if the stars were within her reach. To find that he was only interested in an equitable arrangement—a marriage of convenience, she understood him to mean—came as a bitter disappointment.

"You're overwrought. Perhaps we should discuss this another time."

Would there ever be a good time to offer her marriage in return for providing him with an heir? "Is this how marriages are usually made among Carramer royalty?"

"You know it isn't. I thought…"

She got in first. "That you were doing me a favor?"

He drew himself up, looking terrifyingly regal. "I was going to say that you and I had something good going for us that we could build on for the future, as a family."

He whirled away from her into the suite and she saw him pick up the phone, presumably to order their dinner. Soon she would have to go inside and eat even if it was the last thing she felt like doing. Her doctor had stressed the importance of good nutrition at this time. He'd also told her to avoid stress. Faint hope.

Knowing she would hear when the meal arrived, she remained on the terrace as the dusk gathered around her, trying to order her thoughts. His last words had taken some of the sting out of his proposal, although "something good going for us" hardly translated into the passion of her dreams.

It came to her that his proposal wouldn't hurt so badly if she didn't feel anything for him. All the more reason to put as much distance between them as she could before she did something stupid like saying yes.

Good grief, she was actually considering it. How could she, knowing the baby was what really mattered to him? She pressed her hands to her stomach in an unconsciously protective gesture. Heaven forbid, but what if something went wrong? What would happen to their marriage then? With no divorce in Carramer, they would be bound to one another for all time, without the reason that had brought them together in the first place.

Something between a sob and a laugh welled up, threatening to choke her. As a teenager, she had fantasized about marrying Eduard and having his child. Now he had proposed almost that very thing, and she wanted to run a mile.

She stopped in her tracks. If she married Eduard, her baby would belong to the Carramer royal family, knowing the security and continuity Carissa had wanted all her life. Did she have the right to deny her child that because her ego demanded that she marry for love?

Oh, she had to hand it to Eduard, he was clever. He had left her on her own so she'd think precisely what she was thinking. He knew her so well because she had confided in him with the innocence of youth, little knowing that her confidences would come back to haunt her at this late date.

He knew, because she had told him, how her father's diplomatic lifestyle had made her long for a real home. Now Eduard was offering to provide one for her and her child. The price was a marriage based on friendship rather than love.

She was still debating with herself when she heard Anton arrive, fussily directing a waiter pushing a laden trolley. She gave them a few minutes before going inside. The trolley had been converted into a table, and two chairs had been drawn up to it alongside the French windows. A candle flickered in the center and mouthwatering smells emanated from covered dishes. Anton seated her and flicked a napkin across her lap.

''We'll serve ourselves, thank you, Anton,'' Eduard said.

Anton's speculative look made her face heat, but she kept her head up. ''Let me know when you wish the dinner things removed, Lord Merrisand.''

Eduard nodded, and Anton ushered the waiter ahead of him out of the suite. Carissa glanced at Eduard. From the smooth way he made small talk and uncovered the salvers so she could choose her meal, they could have been two people on a normal date instead of considering marriage.

For she *was* considering it. She probably needed her head examined. Eduard might not love her, but she was dangerously close to loving him. That alone was reason enough to consider his proposal.

But not tonight. As long as he didn't share her feelings, pride demanded that she keep them to herself. She might as well get used to it, she told herself. If they married, she could be doing it for a long time to come.

Chapter Ten

The first thing Carissa noticed next morning was a sense of well-being. It was so novel that she sat up gingerly, testing herself. Her stomach stayed steady. She let a smile blossom. For the first time in weeks, she felt good. Better than good. Terrific.

"Thank you, little one," she murmured, patting her stomach through the thin silk.

The whisper of the fabric reminded her that Eduard had chosen the garment she was wearing. Her smile dimmed further. He had also asked her to marry him. During the oh-so-civilized conversation they'd had about nothing over dinner last night, she had told him she would give him her answer today, after they got back to the lodge. She still didn't know what that answer should be.

She knew what she wanted it to be. Despite everything, she wanted to say yes, but it wasn't that simple. She was no longer an infatuated teenager. She needed to think this through carefully, for her baby's sake and her own.

Not that thinking had helped her last night. Her mind had worried at the question for hours, until she fell into an exhausted sleep. Now, she decided she wasn't going to let the question spoil the best morning she'd had since learning she was pregnant. She flung back the covers. From the bedroom window she could see the river sparkling in the bright Carramer sunshine. Birds swooped and dived above the water. She couldn't wait to go outside and fill her lungs with the sweet air.

By the time she had showered and dressed, Eduard was enjoying orange juice on the terrace. A breakfast trolley had been set up outside, although she hadn't heard it being delivered.

Eduard looked relaxed, but it was a wary kind of relaxation, she noticed, as if he was waiting to hear her response. She was determined not to answer yet, mainly because she didn't know what she was going to say.

It was too soon to say yes and too scary to say no. Follow her mind or her heart? She needed more time, she thought wildly. Last night she had been too stunned to think. Logic threatened to desert her now as she looked at him seated on the banquette, his arm stretched out along the balustrade and one leg crossed over the knee of the other. Every vision she'd ever had of a prince in his castle was embodied in his self-assured pose.

Even the setting supported the vision. She couldn't hear traffic sounds or voices, only the murmur of water and the cries of birds against a backdrop of lush forest and impossibly blue sky.

Lifting her face to the sun, she breathed deeply. If

only she could freeze this moment, keep everything as perfect as it was right now. A foolish hope, she knew, one more worthy of the dreamy teenager he had first known. Everything changed. It would for her, no matter what she decided. For him, too. Her hands curved over her stomach and she mentally apologized to the life inside her. Freezing time would mean denying growth and life to her precious burden, and she wouldn't do that for the world, no matter what the cost to herself.

Eduard got up and poured orange juice for her. When he handed her the glass, he said, "I would have brought you breakfast in bed, but I didn't know how you would be feeling."

A discreet way of telling her he knew how ill she had been every morning. "I feel fine today, just as Dr. Brunet assured me I would, although I was starting to doubt him."

She carried the juice to the edge of the terrace. "It's much too beautiful a morning to lie abed." Although being pampered would have been nice, she thought, imagining Eduard coming into her room with a tray. Too cosily domestic for comfort, she thought, immediately pushing the thought away.

"The trolley's heated so we can eat when you're ready."

Her eyebrow lifted. "Anton thinks of everything." She wondered what he thought of this arrangement, and decided he was probably far too discreet to make any comment. She was the one who felt uncomfortable, which was crazy. They had slept in separate rooms and she doubted if Eduard had lain awake last night, imagining himself in her bed, as she had pictured herself in his.

Watching her, Eduard thought she looked beautiful

this morning. Her hair curled softly around her face, and her gaze was dreamy and faraway. Leaving her to go to his room alone last night had been tougher than anything he'd done in a long time. Seeing her this morning, fresh from bed, made him ache with wanting her. He had to school himself to patience.

He didn't blame her for reacting angrily to his proposal. She thought his only interest was in the baby. In a sense she was right. He wouldn't have proposed to her if she hadn't been pregnant, but it didn't mean he wouldn't have wanted to. Only his sense of justice would have prevented it. How could he ask any woman to marry him when it meant giving up the right to have her own child?

There would be a degree of uproar if Carissa said yes, he accepted. Even in liberal Carramer, members of the royal family were held to higher standards than other people. Announcing his intention to marry a pregnant foreigner would start tongues wagging in earnest. He didn't care. The gossip would die down quickly enough, and he would have Carissa as his wife.

Now that was a future worth considering.

The possibility that she might refuse troubled him. It wasn't that he expected to have his wishes met without question. The navy had disabused him of any such expectations long ago. He *wanted* her in his life. They had made a good team when they were younger, and recent experience at the lodge showed they still did.

The prospect of sharing in the baby's birth, being a father to her child, were undeniably powerful attractions, but it was the thought of possessing Carissa that set his thoughts on fire.

She wouldn't like that word, he chided himself. Satisfying? Satiating? Just working his way through the options sent his temperature climbing. Whatever he called it, he knew his life would be far poorer without her in it.

He refused to think he was in love. No need to confuse things when, in his experience, love didn't last anyway. His experience with Louise, and Carissa's rejection by her baby's father, proved the point. It didn't mean they couldn't base a great relationship on what they did have. All she had to do was agree.

Her sunny smile made his heart beat faster. "I think I'm actually hungry. What have you got hidden in that trolley?" she asked.

He opened the heated cabinet beneath the table, and extracted a platter of scrambled eggs, bacon, mushrooms and tomatoes, as well as a basket of fragrant baked goods. The table was soon crowded with tantalizing offerings. He held a chair out for her with a flourish, enjoying the moment. Enjoying her. "Would madam care to join me?"

Her silvery laughter mingled with the bird calls. "Mademoiselle would."

As Eduard's wife, this could be her life, Carissa told herself, joining him at the table. Not the idyllic surroundings and the pampering, but the sense of togetherness, of belonging to him and to this lovely place. Her need was so overwhelming that she almost said yes there and then. If she hadn't had the baby to consider...

If she hadn't had the baby to consider, he wouldn't have asked her to marry him, she reminded herself. She was no longer anxious to please by falling in with his wishes at the crook of a royal finger. She needed to think about his proposal coolly, balancing the pros against the cons, and arrive at a logical, sensible decision.

With Eduard across the table, offering her delicacies that made her mouth water, she felt neither logical nor sensible. Wearing yesterday's clothes, he managed to look as if he had stepped into them fresh from the hands of a valet. She had the advantage of a new T-shirt, and had rinsed out her underclothes in the bathroom before going to bed, but still couldn't manage his new-minted look. "Do you always look so *together* first thing in the morning?" she asked, annoyed with herself for letting him get to her.

He indicated the sun already well up in the sky. "It's hardly first thing. I'm usually awake at five and can't see any point in going back to sleep."

"Royal habit?" she asked.

His lips curved. "Navy discipline."

She helped herself to more scrambled eggs, added tomatoes and a buttery croissant and made a face at the plain toast. Not needed this morning, thank goodness. "What made you go into the navy?"

He spooned honey onto a croissant and bit into it. After a pause, he said, "Royal sons have a limited range of career choices. I didn't see myself going into government like Mathiaz, so..." His voice trailed off on a shrug.

She wasn't fooled by his offhand tone. "You love the navy, don't you?"

"It's challenging," he said carefully. "Flying is amazing, and there's a chance to make a difference. I don't see the service as a lifetime commitment, but it serves for now."

She swallowed a mouthful of the creamy eggs, wondering if royal brides could have anyone they wanted as their chef. If so, she wanted Anton. Not that she had made a decision yet, she assured herself hastily. It was just nice to dream. "And in the navy you're treated like a normal person," she guessed.

Bull's-eye, she saw when his eyes became hooded, as if she had touched a sensitive spot. "I can't deny it's part of the attraction. I've had to battle all my life for the right to live my life my own way." He gestured around them. "When I told Mathiaz I intended to come to Tiga Falls, he wanted to send a team of bodyguards and palace staff with me."

From what she had seen when he caught up with her con man, Eduard could take care of himself. The knowledge didn't prevent her slight shiver as she thought of all she knew about prominent people being stalked, threatened, even kidnapped. She bit her lip. "Don't you worry about security?"

"I've trained in everything from unarmed combat to defensive driving." He leaned across the table, his fingers brushing her hand. "Does the prospect of a royal lifestyle frighten you, Cris?"

Not as much as the prospect of a marriage without love, she thought. She shook her head. "With a father in the diplomatic service, I had to learn a few things about protecting myself, too. Over the years we lived in some risky places, but Dad believed if you live your life in fear, your enemies have already won."

Eduard nodded his agreement. "Yet you haven't married."

She thought the connection between fear and marriage an odd one, and said so, adding, "I've always assumed I would marry when the time was right."

Was the time right now? he wanted to ask, but held

himself back. "Living the way you did as a child had to be an influence."

She crumbled a piece of croissant between her fingers. "Not having a mother made me less concerned about parents coming in pairs. That's why the prospect of raising my baby alone doesn't alarm me."

Watching the absent way she licked her fingers made the pulse drum in his ears. "You'll make a good mother," he said. A good wife, he wanted to add, but restrained himself. It was killing him not to demand an answer, but royal training made it easier. A de Marigny does not beg, his mother had reminded him more than once, when as a boy, he'd tried to wheedle some favor out of her. Asking Carissa to marry him was hardly begging, so why did her stubborn silence make him want to?

"I hope so," she said softly. She finished her coffee. "Shouldn't we get back to the lodge?"

"There's no hurry. Anton operates the restaurant and the suite as his own business, but this place belongs to the royal family. We can stay as long as we like," he said.

A bright flash of annoyance lit her gaze, making him wish he'd kept his mouth shut. "I wish you'd told me that last night. I'd have insisted on going to the hotel."

Her stiff neck would be the death of him, he decided. What was the difference between sharing the lodge and sharing this apartment? "Good grief, whatever for?" he demanded.

"I'm already far more in your debt than I can repay for a long time."

Her direct gaze met his in fierce challenge. Almost drowning in that molten look, he said hoarsely, "The only debt between us is in your imagination."

"And I can wipe the slate clean by becoming your wife," she said in a voice barely above a whisper.

"One has nothing to do with the other. I didn't ask you to marry me to repay any debt, real or imagined."

"Why did you ask me?"

"Because…" He paused. Had he really almost said, "Because I love you"? Instead, he said, "…I think we're well suited."

Because she could provide him with the child he couldn't otherwise have, she understood as her eyes remained on him. She thought she saw something flicker in his dark gaze, something like a confession, but it was gone as quickly as she noticed it. His face became a regal mask, his true feelings buried as deeply as ever. The price of being royal, she gathered. He had probably been taught to conceal his feelings as soon as he was old enough to appear in public.

If they married, she would have to learn the art, she supposed, as would her child. They would make a happy family, outwardly at least. No one would suspect that the Marquess of Merrisand wasn't loved by her marquis. But she would know.

She blinked hard. "Sometimes being well suited isn't enough. We should go back." She didn't add that in her case, it would be to pack. This interlude had convinced her that the longer she remained under Eduard's roof, the harder it would be to tear herself away. She was already half in love with him. She couldn't risk staying much longer, or she wouldn't have to agonize over his proposal. Saying no was already becoming less of an option. Time she left while the choice existed at all.

Returning to the lodge felt uncomfortably like a homecoming, she thought, as Eduard steered her car into the clearing. A strange car was already parked out front.

"Expecting anyone?" Eduard asked.

Her surprised look flickered to him. "Perhaps it's someone from the police with news about my money."

"Possible, but unlikely. The car has rental plates."

She hadn't noticed. Nor had she seen that a man was sitting in the front seat until he heard them arrive and got out. Eduard helped her out of the car, and her heart began to hammer. There was no mistaking the tall, sandy-haired figure approaching them. "Mark."

His grin brightened and he held out his arms. "Carissa, sweetheart. I've been waiting for over an hour. I was starting to think Jeffrey sent me to the wrong place."

She didn't miss Eduard's frown at Mark's use of the endearment. She dodged the outstretched arms. "Jeff shouldn't have sent you at all."

He had the grace to look abashed. "He didn't actually send me. He only gave me your phone number and told me what you were up to here. I sneaked a look at a postcard you sent him and got the address off that."

Jeff must have had some doubts about telling Mark where she was. Did that mean her brother had begun to suspect Mark's true character? She had sent her brother a card soon after she moved into the lodge. Pride had prevented her from telling her brother how she had been conned out of most of her money, so Mark wouldn't know about that. But she had told him about meeting Eduard again when they talked on the phone, and Jeff must have shared the information with Mark.

Eduard moved up beside her. "I don't believe we've met."

The other man held out his hand. Eduard made no move to take it. Carissa said, "Commander Eduard de Marigny, Marquis of Merrisand, this is Mark Lucas."

Mark's eyebrows flickered in evident surprise. Had she been wrong about his reason for wanting to come? Did he really not know that Eduard was her host? His response to Eduard belied any such notion. "I'm delighted to meet you, Lord Merrisand," he said, inclining his head slightly. "I had no idea that my fiancée was in such distinguished hands."

She felt Eduard grow rigid with tension beside her. "As I had no idea of your relationship."

Something snapped inside her. "Mark has no idea of our relationship either. I am not, and never have been, his fiancée."

"You are carrying my child," the other man said smoothly. "And I do want to marry you."

She had to count to five before she could be sure of responding civilly. "That isn't what you said when I broke the news to you."

"I was in shock, sweetheart. It isn't every day a man finds out he's going to be a father."

Mark couldn't have said anything more cruel in Eduard's hearing, and her heart bled for him, but before she could intervene, he handed her his keys. "I'm going to check on the helicopter while you entertain your guest."

Don't go, not like this, she wanted to cry out. The words choked in her throat. By the time she had herself under some semblance of control, Eduard had rounded the lodge out of sight. She whirled on Mark. "You had no right to come here."

He made a slow perusal of her figure. "The baby gives me the right."

She couldn't listen to any more of this. He had given up any claim on her child when he made his vile suggestion. With shaking hands, she put the key into the lock and pushed the door open. Mark was right behind her, following her into the kitchen before she could stop him.

"Quite a place," he commented, looking around. "You should have told me you had renewed your royal connections."

"And you'd have done what? Pretended you love me so you could make use of my friends?"

"This pregnancy thing is making you too emotional. I don't use people, I make business deals."

"Jeffrey told me you'd lost a great deal of money recently."

He shrugged. "It happens. I'll make it back in one or two good trades."

"Where will the money come from to finance these…trades?"

He hesitated before saying, "Investors."

So she was right. As soon as Mark discovered where she was living and with whom, he had decided to turn the situation to his advantage. It mattered not when he had found out. The result was the same. What would Mark say when she told him that she was merely Eduard's employee, after losing her money through her own foolishness?

"Some coffee would be nice," he said when she didn't offer anything. "Hanging around for an hour was no picnic."

"You didn't have to wait." For want of something better to do, she began to make coffee. Part of her was listening for Eduard's footsteps, hoping he would come in so she could make it clear to him that whatever Mark wanted, she had no part in it.

He didn't come.

Uninvited, Mark had seated himself at the table. She placed a cup of coffee in front of him, not caring that some of it ended up in the saucer. She remained standing.

He left the cup untouched, folding his arms on the table. "I had hoped we could be civilized about this, Carissa, but I can play hardball if you insist."

A tight knot formed in her stomach. "What do you mean?"

"I have as much right to custody of the child as you do."

She knew her color had ebbed, and she gripped the back of a chair. "What do you really want?"

"Clever girl, you know it isn't fatherhood, although if you force me to, I'll swear blind it's my only concern. However, I might lose interest in the baby if you were to persuade your royal lover to invest in my company. Once he comes on board, his name will convince others."

"He isn't..." she began, then stopped as she saw Eduard standing in the doorway. His parade-rest stance made him look like a knight without armor, she thought, blinking away wetness at how hungry she was for the sight of him.

"How much do you want?" he said, in a tone that dripped ice.

Mark seemed unperturbed. He named a figure that made Carissa gasp, but Eduard barely blinked. "How often?"

"I don't understand, Lord Merrisand."

"I think you do. Blackmailers seldom stop at extorting one payment from their victims. How long before you're back demanding more?"

Mark stood up. She didn't blame him. Although only a couple of inches taller than Mark, Eduard managed to give the impression of towering over him. She wondered if he kept his hands behind him to keep them away from Mark's throat.

"Look, this isn't blackmail. It's a business proposition."

Eduard shifted slightly. "That's not how the Carramer courts will regard it."

Mark looked seriously worried now. "You'd have to prove it first."

Slowly, Eduard eased his hands out from behind his back, revealing a portable disk player he must have brought back from his helicopter. "From the moment you threatened to seek custody of Carissa's child, I recorded every word you said. In this country, blackmail is a federal offence."

Mark blanched. Carissa almost felt sorry for him. Almost. Falling over his words, he said, "I love Carissa. I want our child. This is all a misunderstanding."

"And you're the one who made it," Eduard stated. "Now get out before I call the law and give them the recording. If you're out of the country within the next two days, I may see fit to destroy it instead."

Looking as if he could hardly believe he was getting off so lightly, Mark bowed in earnest, but it was a scrabbling effort, as he was moving crabwise toward the door at the same time.

"There's one more thing," Eduard added.

Mark shrank away from Eduard as if the marquis might harm him physically. A distinct possibility, judging from Eduard's murderous expression, Carissa thought. Mark asked sullenly, "What is it?"

"I want a written agreement that you relinquish any claim to Carissa's child now and in the future. The document is to be drawn up and notarized, and couriered to me here before you leave the country."

"You'll have it."

The eagerness she heard in Mark's tone came as a bitter blow. She had known how he felt and should be relieved to know he wouldn't trouble her again, but she couldn't help the bitterness that welled inside her. How could anyone behave so callously toward an innocent life?

The door slammed behind Mark. Moments later, tires screeched on gravel as Mark's car screamed away at high speed.

Her breath whistled out in a rush, and the tears she had held at bay quivered on her lashes. She fought them still, not wanting Eduard to see how close to collapse she felt.

He sensed it and gathered her into his arms. "It's all right, he's gone. I don't think he'll be back, but I'll check with the airport later in the week to make sure he's left the country. If he tries to return at a later date, he'll find he's not welcome in Carramer."

She rested her head against Eduard's shoulder as the tension slowly ebbed out of her. "Thank you for what you did."

He tilted her chin up. "Why didn't you tell me he was threatening you?"

"He wasn't until now. Mark was always an opportunist. Finding out I was staying with you must have given him ideas."

His taut smile reassured her. "I doubt he'll entertain

any more of those ideas for a long time, at least not with you.''

She shifted in his arms, looking at the disk player he'd placed on the table. ''What will you do with the evidence?''

He looked puzzled. ''What?''

''The recording you made of his attempt to blackmail me?'' She didn't like the idea of the conversation being dragged through a court, but the next step was up to Eduard.

His smile widened. ''The court isn't likely to be impressed by a CD of the Carramer Symphony Orchestra.''

She stilled in his arms. ''You were bluffing.''

''The main thing is, Lucas believes it. You're free to make your own choices now.''

His lips moving over her hairline made her wonder just how much freedom she had. She touched her cheek to his. When his mouth reached hers, the breath she drew in tasted of him. She had hoped that by returning to the lodge she could disarm the need for him that raced through her like a lit fuse. Instead, the fire burned more brightly. She couldn't stay around for the inevitable conflagration.

Only a moment more, then she would tell him, she promised herself as he rained kisses down the side of her neck. If she was truly free, he would let her go in peace.

She might go, but she sensed she would know little peace. How could she, after this?

How could her daydreams not be haunted by his gliding touch over her hips, setting off such a clamor of sensations deep inside her that she could hardly breathe. His hands moved lower, cupping her against him and making her aware that he was no more immune than she was.

Unable to resist, she linked her arms around his neck, leaving barely a breath of space between them. He took her mouth again with an urgency she felt all the way to the soles of her feet. They weren't touching the ground, she realized. She was held up by his embrace.

"Eduard."

The alarm in her voice broke through the fog in his brain. He eased her gently to her feet and stepped back. "Did I hurt you? Is it the baby?"

Always his concern was for the baby. The disappointment made it easier to say, "No, I'm not hurt." Not in the way he meant, anyway. "This isn't right."

Horrified by how close he'd just come to taking what he wanted without considering her needs, he nodded. "It isn't the way I want it to happen, either." Moonlight, roses, champagne, soft music. He wanted them all for her, to set the scene when he made her his, so she would remember their first time as special, not as a moment of mindless passion that consumed where it touched.

She shook her head. "That isn't what I mean. I have to go, Eduard."

A fierce pain stabbed through him, a forewarning that he wasn't going to like this. "You want to rest?"

"I have to leave."

He could hardly force the word out. "When?"

"Soon. I have to find a job and a home, and get back on my feet before the baby comes."

"You don't have to. You could stay with me. As my wife."

The bleakness in his expression almost destroyed her

until she reminded herself that he didn't want a wife, he wanted a child. "I can't. I'm sorry."

Her defenses were too fragile. Before he could say anything more to undermine them, she walked out of the room, steeling herself not to look back.

Chapter Eleven

Three days later, she was still living at the lodge. The local real estate agent had been unable to help her find rental accommodation in the area, and the receptionist at the Monarch Hotel regretfully explained that they were closing for renovation work. As a last resort, she had contacted the Rain Forest Resort cabins where she and Eduard had located Dominic Hass, but they had no vacancies for some weeks.

"With the hotel closed, the cabins will be very popular," the manager explained in a tone tinged with apology. "I can let you know as soon as something becomes available."

"Thank you," she said. She left her number and hung up with a sigh. She hadn't had much luck with the people who had promised earlier to consider her as an employee, either. Even those who had been encouraging when she'd called them before now sounded offhand when she spoke with them. It seemed she had no choice but to look farther afield.

Perhaps it was for the best. No matter how attractive she found the area, staying nearby, knowing she could run into Eduard at any time, would have made her life a misery. She had to face the fact that she was in love with him. Trying to call it by some other, less daunting name didn't change reality. She had started loving him when she was fifteen and had never stopped.

Several times in the last couple of days she had been tempted to say she had changed her mind and would marry him. Then she had made herself remember what it was like to grow up with a father who did his duty by her, but shared nothing of his emotions. Her child was going to have a father who loved them both. She would accept nothing less.

She blinked angrily. The wetness on her cheeks had nothing to do with Eduard.

She had been making the calls from his study, doodling idly on a daily calendar on his desk. Flipping back through the week she stilled, her gaze riveted by the notes she had just uncovered.

In Eduard's distinctive handwriting were the names and numbers of the Monarch Hotel, the Rain Forest Resort, their managers and a number of the employment resources in the area that she had tried without success. A horrible suspicion began to dawn, and with it a growing sense of betrayal.

Without giving herself time to cool down, she stormed out of the study in search of him. She found him tinkering with the helicopter engine. In dark-brown chinos and a matching polo shirt, he looked less like a knight of the realm, and more like the boy next door. The very handsome, virile boy next door. Except that no one with any power of observation could call him a boy.

She ignored the sudden fast beating of her heart and the almost overpowering desire to lose herself in his comforting arms. Not while she was mad as the furies at him.

He heard her coming and straightened, wiping oily hands on a rag. "How's it going?"

She wasn't fooled by his air of innocence. Nor was she going to be sidetracked by the warmth that surged through her when he turned his high-voltage smile on her.

"You tell me."

His eyebrows arched, the smile easing back a little. Not enough to stop heat from racing along her veins and pooling somewhere around her heart. "I gather you're still having no luck with your quest?"

"No. Thanks to you."

He let the rag drop and ducked under the rotors to her side. "How did this get to be my fault?"

"Do you deny sabotaging my efforts to find a job and somewhere else to live?"

His silence spoke volumes. "You credit me with a lot of power," he said after a time.

"You *have* a lot of power. All the Marquis of Merrisand has to do is spread the word that he'd rather Miss Day didn't find what she was looking for, and everyone falls in with his royal wishes. But it isn't going to work. You aren't going to make me stay."

He lifted his hands as if about to touch her, then let them drop to his sides. Something like disappointment jolted through her. What was going on here? She had stormed outside wanting his blood, but the impulse vanished as soon as she set eyes on him, replaced by a desire that was far harder to fight. She wanted his touch as much as she wanted to keep breathing. The last three days had been sheer torture, sharing the same roof with him and trying to keep her distance.

Maybe they should just make love and get it over with. The thought rocked her to her core, but it wasn't the answer. Once she had shared his bed, she would never find the strength to walk away.

She wondered if he knew it, and was hoping to buy time to bind her to him with ties of…not love, not on his side, but lust, anyway. What it would be on her side didn't bear thinking about.

"Would it help if I say I want you to stay?" he asked.

No news there. "I've told you why I can't."

He rested a hand on the helicopter's clear canopy. "You haven't, not really."

Elementally aware of him, she took a half step back and said the first thing that came into her head. "It can't work between us. What if I decide I want more children, Eduard?" Phrasing it as a question saved her from telling an outright lie. She would accept him on any terms at all if it meant she could have his love. But that wasn't what he was offering.

She regretted the misdirection when she saw his eyes turn smoky, but she couldn't take it back. He sounded cold and distant as he said, "I see."

She tried to justify her action as self-defense, but felt as low as she had ever done. "Will you tell the people you called to stop giving me the brush-off?"

He shook his head. "I shan't put any more obstacles in your way, but I won't help you to leave me, Cris. I'm not that big a masochist."

He turned back to his work, the conversation clearly ended. She watched him for a few minutes, biting her tongue to stop herself from telling him it was all a lie.

She didn't want more children. She didn't want to hurt him in any way. All she wanted was his love.

Since it wasn't going to happen in her lifetime, she stiffened her shoulders and spun around. Before she could take a step, he said over his shoulder, "I have some news for you. The police have retrieved your money. You'll get it back as soon as the police complete their investigation. I intended to tell you over dinner tonight, but you may as well know now."

He didn't look at her. Her delight at the news was dampened by his flat delivery. She felt as if she had spoiled a treat, like the time she'd stumbled across her Christmas presents hidden in her father's suitcase when she was seven. Instead of being excited, she had felt sick with disappointment, as if she had personally killed Santa Claus. "That's wonderful," she said, sounding as flat as he did. "Thank you."

He didn't respond, so she walked slowly back to the lodge. She should be happy. Eduard's news had given her a reprieve. Instead of looking for somewhere to rent, she could buy her bed-and-breakfast place, as she had planned.

Except that her plans hadn't included falling in love.

"It's just you and me now," she said, her voice catching as she skimmed her palm over her stomach. "We'll find the perfect place, and we'll be happy together, won't we?"

Annoyed with herself, she grabbed her bag. The best way to get Eduard out of her system was to give herself a new focus. She would drive out to the house she had intended to look at before she met Dominic Hass. Having, as she thought, agreed to buy the lodge, she had never gone to inspect the first property. Now was as good a time as any, providing it was still on the market.

When she had inquired about it originally, the selling agent hadn't been able to take her to see it right away, and had given her directions, suggesting she look at the outside and decide if she wanted to see through it later.

That was how she'd ended up in her present predicament, she recalled with a grimace. If the agent for the first house had been free, she wouldn't have become involved with the lodge—or Eduard.

She wasn't involved with him. She was useful. Big difference. One hand diving into her bag for her keys, she hurtled out of the back door and into her car. She decided against telling Eduard where she was going, in case the other property became mysteriously unavailable. He had said he wouldn't interfere, but she wasn't taking any chances.

The agent's driving directions were still at the bottom of her purse. She dug them out and started the car. Eduard had the helicopter engine turning over, the sound covering her departure.

She wasn't sure where she took the wrong turning, but after fifteen minutes' driving, she found herself on a bumpy dirt road that looked more like a fire trail than the access to anywhere. Unless the owner of the property was a hermit, she was lost.

Without warning, the road ended at a thick stand of rain forest. Getting out to look, she wasn't unduly worried. Her cell phone was in her bag. If she called Eduard and described her location, he would probably be able to guide her back to the right road. It would mean explaining what she was doing so she decided to save that option until she had exhausted all others.

Not that she had many to choose from. Off to her right was a narrow path ending in a faded sign. Reading it might tell her where she was. She stopped at the car long enough to holster her water bottle on her hip, then set off. The sign was no more than a hundred yards away.

Before she had covered half the distance, she felt the ground give way beneath her. She scrabbled at bushes beside the track but they shredded in her grasp, lacerating her hands as she slid, then fell into the darkness below, bushes and rocks tumbling after her.

She landed on her back, snagging her hip on a jagged outcropping of rock, the breath driving out of her. For a few seconds all she could do was lie still, trying to get her breath back, shielding her head from the debris raining down on her. When it stopped, she cautiously moved her arms and legs. Everything worked. By a miracle, she hadn't broken anything in the fall. She sat up.

A sharp pain shot through her lower back and she caught her lip between her teeth. Hoping she was only bruised, she moved more slowly to get to her feet, hanging on to the outcrop for support. Her legs felt like jelly.

"We've sure done it this time," she said to the life inside her, her voice shaking with horror. If the fall had hurt her baby… She resisted the thought. Her child was going to be all right. She wouldn't let herself believe anything else.

She looked around. She was in a rock fissure that had been roofed over by a crust of leaves and branches until she had broken through it. A shaft of sunlight lit the fissure, enough to show her that she wasn't getting out the way she came in. The crumbled roof was too far over her head, and the walls offered few footholds for climbing. Water pooled in places on the sloping floor. She wouldn't die of thirst anyway. Just as well because her water bottle had shattered, the contents soaking the legs of her jeans.

In the dimness, she saw markings on the walls of the fissure. The stick figures looked ancient and she remembered Eduard telling her that this area was full of caves used centuries before by the Mayat people.

She shivered as much with fear and pain as with the cave's chill. Why hadn't she told Eduard where she was going? It could be nightfall before he came looking for her, and the rain forest was a big place. The thought that she might never see him again plunged her into despair. If any harm had befallen her baby, he wouldn't want her anyway. That should be reason enough for her to harden her heart against him. But all she could think of was how cruel it would be if she died here without ever having the chance to tell him she loved him.

There had to be something she could do.

A fire. If she could make one, she could direct smoke out of the hole in the roof as a signal. Strewn around the cave were the bits of twigs and branches that had accompanied her fall. Some had landed in the water, but enough remained dry to give her hope. She had never been a Girl Scout, but had seen enough survival programs to know she had to rub one of the dry sticks against another until she got a spark, then feed the flame with the dry leaves.

And hope Eduard came looking for her and noticed the smoke.

Lunchtime had been and gone by the time Eduard decided to take a break. The chopper engine sounded much sweeter for his attention. He enjoyed getting his hands dirty occasionally, but today the task was as much to distract himself as because the chopper needed the work.

It was killing him not to tell Carissa she had to marry him because he loved her too much to let her go. But she wanted more children, the one reason he wouldn't tell her how he felt. How he'd felt since they were teenagers and she was way off-limits to him. She was still off-limits because he wasn't about to let her sacrifice her dream for him.

Seeing her car missing brought him up short. His heart felt as if a tight fist had clenched around it. Had she left him already? Telling himself it was for the best failed to calm him. He strode inside, calling her name, knowing it was stupid, but feeling a huge weight shift off his shoulders when he found her stuff still in her bedroom.

Where could she be? They weren't out of anything and she hadn't mentioned any problems.

The baby.

The fist clenched tighter until he forced himself to breathe. Had something gone wrong? Why in blazes hadn't she alerted him? Eduard had to know, to be there for her, whether she wanted him to or not.

He was out of the house and climbing into the chopper before he had the thought fully hatched. Moments later he was orbiting the clearing and heading over the trees in the direction of the town. The moves were automatic, leaving him free to scan the ground for signs of her car.

He spotted it where he least expected it, at the end of an old fire trail about fifteen minutes away from the lodge, still on crown land. What was she doing there? The only landmark near that trail was an ancient Mayat cave system that his father had arranged to have sign-posted years ago to deter his sons from exploring the dangerously crumbling labyrinth.

Eduard chilled, thinking of his father's stern warning to keep away from the caves. The area was riddled with them and the Mayat had guarded some with hidden traps to protect their sacred sites. If Carissa had blundered into one of them— A wisp of smoke curling between the trees interrupted the thought. Fire? No, a signal. She *was* down there. He had to get to her.

The fire trail was the only place flat enough to land the chopper, and it was barely wide enough to support the length of the skids. Using every ounce of training and skill he'd acquired, he settled the aircraft inch by inch, watching for rocks and objects which could have spelled disaster, releasing a huge breath when he made it down safely.

He didn't wait for the rotors to stop spinning but ducked under them at a run and headed for the source of the smoke. He didn't have to go far to see what had happened. A natural fissure running away from the main cave had opened up, probably right under her feet. His blood ran cold, thinking of her falling all that way. He had to remind himself that the smoke meant she was alive. He cupped his hands around his face and called her name.

"Down here." Her voice though faint, sounded strong and glad to see him.

Not as glad as he was. He dropped full length and peered over the rim of the crater until he could see her in the gloom below. She was holding a handful of the dry leaves she'd evidently been using to feed a tiny fire. "Are you hurt?"

She dropped the leaves and looked up. "Only bruised, I think. I can't find a way out."

"Leave that to me."

A few minutes later he was back with a coil of rope ladder from the chopper. A huge old ironwood tree at the edge of the trail provided an anchor point. "Stand back," he instructed.

After he made sure she was clear, he hurled the coil into the crater. It swung to within a few inches of her head. He tested the anchor points then began to climb down, jumping the last stretch. "How are you at rope climbing?"

She looked uncertain. "I flunked gym at school."

He hooked an arm around her waist. "This time you're going to pass with flying colors."

In his arms she felt wonderful. Under different circumstances, he would have been tempted to make the most of being alone with her in the dim coolness of the cave. But he hadn't missed her gasp of pain when he touched her back.

As carefully as he could, he lifted her up and she grasped the ladder. It swung wildly and took all his strength to hold steady for her. "Hook your arms and legs around the side ropes," he instructed. "Then climb straight up, one rung at a time. Don't look down."

He didn't breathe again until she reached the top and hauled herself over the rim of the crater. She made only the tiniest whimper, but the sound tore at his gut. He followed her up the ladder in double time, not caring how many times he careened against the side walls. That whimper had him terrified.

She sat on the ground away from the crater lip, legs drawn up and her head resting on her knees. He knelt beside her, his heart in overdrive. "What is it? Good grief, you're soaking wet."

When she lifted her head, her eyes were cloudy with pain. "I shattered a water bottle when I fell."

He swept her into his arms, ignoring her protests. His heart drummed so loudly it was a wonder she couldn't hear it. "I'm getting you to the hospital right now."

She linked her arms around his neck. "I'm all right, really."

He wished he was as sure. No water bottle he'd ever seen leaked red fluid. He didn't know what it meant, but he was sure it couldn't be anything good.

How long did it take to find out whether or not a woman had lost her baby? Eduard paced the waiting room at the hospital in Casmira, feeling as if he was in danger of wearing a track in the carpet.

He had radioed ahead, obtaining permission to land at the hospital's pad. A team from the emergency room had met them there, taking immediate charge of Carissa who by then was groggy, although still denying that anything was the matter.

"How about we let the professionals decide?" he'd said, grasping her hand.

Then she was whisked away, and he was left to wear out the carpet. He should be thankful he had the room to himself, a courtesy accorded his position, he knew. As soon as he had identified himself on the radio, the hospital had rolled out the metaphorical red carpet. He didn't object to the fuss as long as it got Carissa the attention she needed.

She hadn't said much on the way to the hospital, but he'd known she was in pain and had tried to keep from jolting her as much as possible, setting the chopper down as lightly as he could. All the way he'd berated himself for using the rope ladder instead of a basket or a harness to lift her out of the cave. What sort of monster was he to expect an injured woman to climb out under her own steam?

A monster who loved her, simple as that. With or without child, on any terms at all, he loved her and wanted her in his life. It tore at him that he couldn't tell her, but he knew it was the ultimate act of love, to let her go when everything in him ached to keep her with him.

He jerked around as a white-coated woman came into the room. "Lord Merrisand, you can see Miss Day now."

"Is she all right?" He couldn't bring himself to ask about the baby.

The woman smiled but it was one of those medical, tell-you-nothing smiles meant to reassure, when all it did was set his pulse hammering. "Why don't you see for yourself."

How bad could things be if they were letting her have visitors? he asked himself as his long legs ate up the corridor between the waiting room and the private suite he'd arranged for Carissa. Realizing he was empty-handed, he choked back a laugh. He'd flown her in from the wilderness. She wouldn't expect grapes and flowers.

He wanted them for her. He wanted to call the hospital florist and clean out their entire stock to fill her room with the beauty she deserved. But he couldn't take the time now. He had to see her. As he cruised past the nurses' station, he settled for scooping up a vase of tropical orchids en passant. The nurse on duty opened her mouth to object, took one look at his face and broke into a grin.

At the door of Carissa's suite he dragged in a steadying breath and went in.

She was sitting up against a bank of pillows, looking pale and tired. He was relieved to see she wasn't hooked up to anything. That had to be a good sign, surely? Her hair was brushed back from her face, and violet shadows rimmed her eyes.

He placed the vase of orchids on the bedside chest. "These are for you."

She reached for the card tucked into the blooms. "Thank you...Lionel."

He returned her smile sheepishly. "I didn't want to take the time to get some of my own. Are you all right?"

She nodded, easing herself away from the pillow and wincing. "The doctor says I bruised my spine when I landed, but otherwise I'm fine."

"But the bleeding..."

"I gashed my leg on an outcrop on the way down. They've given me something for it, and they assure me it isn't serious."

"Thank heavens. I've been going out of my mind."

She knew the baby was his main concern, although she didn't let him see how much the knowledge hurt. He hadn't pretended anything else when he proposed, so she shouldn't be surprised. It didn't change the powerful sense of love she felt for him, futile though it was.

Eduard sat on the edge of her bed and leaned across to kiss her. This time she was surprised, but of course he was as relieved as she was that nothing had gone wrong. All the same, her heart began an insistent flutter that left her breathless.

He caught her hands and brought them to his lips.

"When I saw your car on the fire trail, I was worried sick."

She struggled to ignore the heat igniting inside her at his touch. "What made you come looking for me?"

"You left without telling me where you were going. I thought something was wrong."

"With the baby?" Nothing else would have brought him in search of her.

He nodded, still holding her hands. "Was that why you left?"

Her lashes fluttered over damp eyes. "I was going to inspect a house, the one I meant to look at before I met Dominic Hass."

"You really meant to leave?"

It was true, but she wished she didn't have to tell him like this, and have to face the burning disappointment in his gaze. She knew he was only concerned for the baby, and wanted to weep. "I'm sorry, Eduard, but I can't stay, knowing how you feel about me."

A frown shadowed his forehead. "I hoped you were starting to feel the same way."

She blinked hard. "What are you saying?"

"I'm trying to tell you I love you. Isn't that what you meant when you said you know how I feel?" He wouldn't have spoken out otherwise.

"You didn't love me until you found out I was pregnant," she pointed out.

He got up unsteadily and began to prowl around the spacious suite. "Is that why you believe I proposed to you?"

Her gaze followed him, more hungry than she liked. "Isn't it?"

"Well, yes, but not for the reason you think." He stopped moving and feasted his eyes on her. "Before

I knew about the baby, I told myself I didn't have the right to ask you—or any woman—to marry me when we couldn't have children of our own.''

She moistened her lips. "And if we could?"

His gaze darkened. "Nothing on earth would have stopped me from declaring my love for you. When I saw you again at the lodge, the years fell away and I remembered all the reasons I was attracted to you when we were teenagers. I didn't know how to show you then, but I do now."

He slid onto the bed beside her and gathered her into his arms. She went willingly, still not sure what was happening between them, but willing to trust him. He kissed her long and deeply, making her head spin. "Say you'll marry me, Cris. I love you. I'm sorry as hell about what happened. I know how much you wanted this baby, but we'll get through the loss together somehow, I promise."

She had trouble believing what she was hearing. He thought she had lost the baby, yet he still loved her and wanted to marry her. Happiness flooded through her until she could hardly breathe. "When I thought I was trapped in the cave, the hardest thing was thinking I would lose you, too, before I could tell you how much I love you."

He lifted his head, his eyes bright. "Then your answer is yes?"

No other answer was possible. "Yes, oh yes. But there's something else you should know." His arms tightened around her in silent support as she said, "I'm still pregnant."

He took a moment to absorb her words, then he let out a whoop of joy. "You mean...?"

She nodded, unaccountably shy. "I'm waiting for

news of some tests, but the doctor assures me there was no miscarriage.''

He rained kisses over her upturned face, his eyes suspiciously moist. ''Darling, you've made me the happiest man alive—twice over.''

No happier than he made her. He loved her. He wanted her for herself. How could she ever have doubted him? She made a promise never to do it again, as she cradled his head against her, overwhelmed by happiness. ''It seems the Mayat spirits at the falls knew a thing or two after all.''

He gave her a baffled look. ''The spirits?''

She smiled, remembering. ''When we visited Tiga Falls, you told me the legend that the spirits borrow energy from us, and give love in return. It seems you were right.''

He stroked her hair. ''Who am I to argue with a legend?''

A discreet cough made Eduard pull away from her. Looking not in the least concerned, he turned to the doctor. ''What is it?''

The woman's face was red. ''Sorry to interrupt, but I have the results of your tests.''

Carissa gripped Eduard's hand hard. ''Is there a problem with the baby?''

''Babies,'' the doctor said, coming closer. ''I wanted a second opinion to be sure, but you're having triplets, and they're all fine.''

Carissa felt the bed whirl around her. ''Three babies? Oh, my.''

Eduard looked as if he wanted to stand up and beat his chest. ''We're going to have three children?''

''A ready-made family,'' Carissa agreed, her heart

bursting with love for him. His expression said it all. She could have given him no greater gift.

But she was wrong. "This is the icing on the cake," he said. He grinned at the doctor. "You're the first to know that Carissa has just agreed to marry me."

"Congratulations," she said, looking bemused.

"We have to tell Prince Josquin before we can make it official," he added.

"I'll keep the news under doctor-patient confidentiality," the doctor agreed, the sparkle in her eyes belying her serious demeanor. "I hope you'll be very happy."

"Count on it." Eduard pulled Carissa to him as the door swung closed. "The way I feel right now, I don't think there's a happier person in the whole kingdom of Carramer than me."

Laughing through a mist of happy tears, Carissa shook her head. "I can think of one. Or is that four?" Finding that she was carrying triplets was going to take some getting used to, she decided.

Eduard didn't seem to be having any difficulty. "If they're all as beautiful and sweet as their mother, who's counting?"

Epilogue

A triple christening had to be a first for the Carramer royal family, Carissa thought as she walked up the aisle of the beautiful chapel at Merrisand Castle. In her arms she cradled her son, Jamet, the oldest by a few minutes. Beside her, Eduard carried their daughter, Michelle. On his other side walked the babies' godparents, Princess Sarah and Prince Josquin, the prince holding tiny Henry gingerly in his arms. All three babies were asleep for the moment, but if one woke up, they all would, then it would be bedlam, she knew from recent experience.

"Tell Josquin he won't break Henry if he holds him a little more tightly," she murmured to Eduard.

Her husband grinned back. "He's had more practice at this than I have."

Josquin was regent for his adopted son, Christophe, the heir to the Valmont throne. Right now the heir had his hand tucked in his mother's as he toddled up the aisle beside his parents.

Josquin was unlikely to have had more practice at caring for babies than she and Eduard these past few weeks, she thought. No one would have thought it unusual if they had entrusted the triplets entirely to the care of royal nannies, but by unspoken agreement, they had chosen to be hands-on parents.

Perhaps it was knowing how precious these babies were to him, but Eduard had hardly been able to bring himself to leave them since they were born. She suspected that Prince Josquin had influenced the navy to grant Eduard extended leave to be with his new family. If he hadn't, Eduard might well have gone AWOL because she suspected nothing was going to tear him away from them for some time to come.

He still carried out his duties as part of the Merrisand Trust, but he worked in his study in the family apartments at the castle. They had set up home there after she was forced to leave the work at Tiga Falls Lodge in other hands when her advancing pregnancy made rest imperative. Much as she had enjoyed seeing her vision for the lodge become reality, she was happy to let the designers Eduard appointed finish the task. The lodge would not be officially open for some months. They would still have it to themselves for a family holiday after the christening.

Eduard had been at her side when the babies were born, helped into the world by Dr. Brunet, under the watchful eye of the court physician, Alain Pascale. Even the somewhat irascible doctor had struggled to stay dry-eyed as, one after another, the triplets announced their arrival with lusty cries. Carissa and Eduard had barely drawn breath since.

Eduard had quickly become adept at bathing slippery bodies, changing them and crooning a Carramer lullaby to them at bedtime. No man could make a more loving father than Eduard.

Not that she felt left out. He had gone to great lengths to assure her she would always be his first love. Even without his reassurance, she would have known it from the tender way his gaze rested on her when he thought she didn't notice, and from the thoughtful little things he did for her at every opportunity: chocolates on her pillow at night, a flower by her place at the table, his hand slipping into hers when they took the babies for walks around the castle grounds. They made quite a convoy, but Eduard managed to make her feel as if they were alone together.

Her eyes misted as she remembered walking down this same aisle to be married to him, surrounded by his family and her brother, Jeffrey, and an awesome gathering of the world's key figures. She had had eyes for no one but Eduard.

He had used his influence to arrange the ceremony quickly, as if afraid that she would vanish if he took his eyes off her. As if she would. Having found heaven, one didn't willingly walk out on it. And she had known that's what she had found when she saw him, resplendent in his dress whites, turn to watch her approach. The love in his gaze had taken her breath away. Nothing he had done or said since had given her cause to doubt how deeply she was loved.

They had left the chapel under a ceremonial arch of swords held by Eduard's naval colleagues. Today there would be no swords, but bells would ring throughout the province to mark the christening of the three royal children.

"Happy, *ma amouvere?*" Eduard asked softly, using the most intimate of Carramer endearments.

Too choked to speak, she nodded. She let her gaze drift to the other members of the congregation. Carramer's monarch, Prince Lorne, Eduard's cousin, was there with his family. His brother, Michel, was holding hands with Princess Caroline, like the lovers they still were. Beside them, their two children watched the proceedings with fascination. Little Daniel, the son of Lorne's sister, Adrienne, and her husband, Hugh, was tugging at the collar of his tiny suit. So was Hugh, Carissa noticed, hiding a smile. She would have to warn Eduard that their children were likely to mimic their habits, and not always the preferred ones.

Mathiaz and his wife, Jacinta, were talking softly to Mathiaz and Eduard's parents. They had welcomed Carissa into their family as a daughter no less generously than they had done when she was a teenager.

Her brother had flown in from Sydney a few days ago. Jeff had apologized for trying to steer her toward Mark, whose true nature he had finally faced, and with whom he had severed all ties. She nodded to several members of the diplomatic community who had known her family while they lived in Carramer. Only one person was missing—her father. He would have been proud of her and his grandchildren, she felt certain. Her gaze blurred and she turned to Eduard again as they took their places at the front of the chapel.

Henry opened his eyes and started to wail. "Has to make sure he has everyone's attention, just like his namesake," Josquin said, his proud expression taking any sting out of his words.

To Carissa's amazement, the other babies slept on for the moment. Looking at her son being rocked in Prince Josquin's arms, she smiled. "You don't regret naming Henry after your uncle, do you?'' In another few minutes it would be too late to change their minds.

Her husband shook his head. ''Prince Henry was a bit of a tyrant, but he had his people's best interests at heart. His family's too. I'll never forget that his legacy made our love possible and enabled us to become a family.''

A family. How wonderful that sounded, she thought, her shimmering gaze flying to her husband. Had Henry not bequeathed Tiga Falls Lodge to Eduard, they might never have fallen in love. It was only fitting that the last-born of their children carry Henry's name as a reminder of all he had done for her and Eduard.

They weren't the only ones whose happiness had flowed from Henry's legacy, she knew. Eduard had explained how Henry had brought Josquin and Sarah together by naming Christophe as his heir and appointing Josquin regent. The heirloom ring he had bequeathed to Mathiaz in his will had led to the romance between Eduard's brother and his one-time bodyguard, Jacinta.

Three legacies, three enduring loves, she thought. All were the gifts of one extraordinary man. Her new family was renowned for extraordinary people who had ruled this wonderful country for a thousand years. Now her children were part of that continuum. They were part of Carramer as she was, loved as she was. Prince Henry had made the miracle possible, and she sent him a silent message of thanks. Eduard took her arm, his touch testifying to how well he understood.

Carissa had finally come home.

* * * * *

Silhouette Romance presents tales of
enchanted love and things beyond explanation
in the heartwarming series

Soulmates

Couples destined for each other are brought
together by the powerful magic of love....

Broken hearts are healed
WITH ONE TOUCH
by Karen Rose Smith (on sale January 2003)

Love comes full circle when
CUPID JONES GETS MARRIED
by DeAnna Talcott (on sale February 2003)

Soulmates

Some things are meant to be....

*Available at
your favorite retail outlet.*

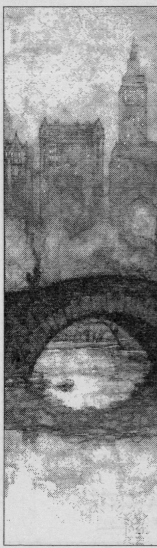

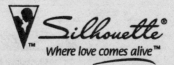

If you enjoyed what you just read,
then we've got an offer you can't resist!

Take 2 bestselling
love stories FREE!
Plus get a FREE surprise gift!

eHARLEQUIN.com

community | membership

buy books | authors | online reads | magazine | learn to write

buy books

Your one-stop shop for great reads at great prices.
We have all your favorite Harlequin, Silhouette,
MIRA and Steeple Hill books, as well as a host of
other bestsellers in Other Romances. Discover a
wide array of new releases, bargains and hard-to-
find books today!

learn to write

Become the writer you always knew you could be:
get tips and tools on how to craft the perfect
romance novel and have your work critiqued by
professional experts in romance fiction. Follow
your dream now!

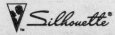

Silhouette®

Where love comes alive™—online...

Visit us at
www.eHarlequin.com

SINTLTW

SILHOUETTE *Romance*

COMING NEXT MONTH

#1636 THE CINDERELLA INHERITANCE—Carolyn Zane
Cynthia Noble inherited a mansion from her fiancé's grandfather—
and was branded a gold digger as a result! Intent on uncovering his
future sister-in-law's true motives, Rick Wingate followed Cynthia's
every move. But would he prove Cynthia was the perfect wife for his
brother—or for himself?

#1637 SLEEPING BEAUTY & THE MARINE—Cathie Linz
Street-smart reporter Cassie Jones didn't have time for romantic
dreams or cocky flyboy Sam Wilder! Her journalism career demanded
she feature the handsome U.S. Marine captain in a story. But when did
"up close and personal" start including Sam's passionate kisses?

#1638 WITH ONE TOUCH—Karen Rose Smith
Soulmates
Veterinarian Nate Stanton realized there was more to beautiful
Brooke Pennington than met the eye—and it was wreaking havoc on
his emotions. Brooke knew her solitude-seeking employer would never
understand her extraordinary gift—nor live with the complications it
brought. So why wasn't she running from *his* special touch?

#1639 BABY ON BOARD—Susan Meier
Daycare Dads
Caro Evans didn't want to accompany Max Riley to bring his abandoned
infant daughter home—much less be attracted to the confounding but
oh-so-sexy man! Wanting to be a good father, Max enrolled in Caro's
Single Dad School. Now, if he could only convince his lovely teacher to
give him some one-on-one lessons after class....

#1640 THE PRINCE'S TUTOR—Nicole Burnham
Stefano diTalora had always run wild—until his father hired stunning
Amanda Hutton to teach him appropriate palace behavior. Shaken by the
seductive, virile prince, Amanda vowed to keep Stefano out of trouble—
but the job description said nothing about keeping him out of her heart!

#1641 THE VIRGIN'S PROPOSAL—Shirley Jump
The first time Katie Dole met rebel-with-a-cause Matt Webster, she
was clad in a banana suit. The second time, she convinced him to pose
as her fiancé! Matt was hardly marriage material, but with every passionate kiss Matt found himself going bananas—over Katie!

SRCNM1202